The Dream Weavers

The Dream Weavers

Short stories by the nineteenth-century
Pre-Raphaelite poet-painters

William Morris   Dante Gabriel Rossetti
Algernon Charles Swinburne   Edward Burne-Jones
William Fulford   R. W. Dixon

With an introduction by John Weeks

Published by
Woodbridge Press Publishing Company
Santa Barbara, California 93111

Published by

Woodbridge Press Publishing Company
Post Office Box 6189
Santa Barbara, California 93111

Published simultaneously in the United States and Canada

Printed in the United States of America

Library of Congress Cataloging in Publication Data

Main entry under title:
The Dream weavers.

"A Banquo book."

CONTENTS: Swinburne, A. C. The marriage of Mona Lisa.—Swinburne, A. C. Dead love.—Swinburne, A. C. The portrait.—Rossetti, D. G. The orchard pit.—Rossetti, D. G. Saint Agnes of Intercession. [etc.]
    1. Short stories—English. I. Weeks, John, 1949-   II. Pre-Raphaelite Brotherhood.
PZ1.D6542   [PR1309.S5]   823'.01   79-26749
ISBN 0-912800-73-9

The cover:

"Hylas and the Nymphs," by John William Waterhouse
Courtesy of City of Manchester Art Gallery

Contents

Introduction

These are stories of strange beauty by men of strange genius, the nineteenth-century Pre-Raphaelites, painters who were also poets who were also sculptors and architects and designers and craftsmen.

It should not be surprising that the Pre-Raphaelites also turned their hand to the short story form, and that like their pictures and poems their stories are things of startling beauty and vivid imagination. And yet it is surprising, in a world which continues to value Pre-Raphaelite art and which values more than it once did the imaginative forms of literature, that these stories are almost unknown. They are collected here for the first time.

The Pre-Raphaelite Brotherhood was formed in September, 1848, by three young English painters, students at the Royal Academy, who determined to defy the Academy standard of art, still patterned upon the stylized religious painting of the High Renaissance. They resolved to create a new art, modeled upon the more naturalistic style of painting which in their estimation had antedated Raphael.

William Holman Hunt, 1827-1910, believed in the truth of nature and the morality of art with the intensity of an Old Testament prophet, an intensity which grew during a long lifetime into religious obsession and drove him repeatedly to the Holy Land.

John Everett Millais, 1829-1896, was a brilliantly gifted craftsman who ultimately yielded to convention and success, became a baronet and president of the Royal Academy and died England's most famous and possibly richest painter.

Dante Gabriel Rossetti, 1828-1881, was a finer poet than a painter, a charismatic manipulator of men and women but a slave of love, or rather his own notion of love, which was a destructive paradox of the ideal, the illicit and the impossible. He died a tragic figure, neurotic, reclusive and drug-addicted.

A second generation of Pre-Raphaelites surrounded Rossetti in the middle 1850s, after the short-lived original Brotherhood had broken up. There was Algernon Charles Swinburne, 1837-1909, who had one of the sweetest tongues and most perverted minds in English poetry, Edward Burne-Jones, 1833-1898, who became a much greater painter than his master Rossetti, and William Morris, 1834-1896, a dynamic man of Promethean talents and accomplishments who wrote immensely popular poetry, revolutionized the decorative arts, pioneered British socialism and in the last years of his life wrote long prose romances, prototypes of the modern literary genre of fantasy. Morris was also the husband of the enthrallingly beautiful Jane Burden, who became the model and stereotype of the languorous damozel in Pre-Raphaelite painting, and became as well the adulterous lover of Rossetti.

This is only a cast of major characters. In fact, the Pre-Raphaelite movement included many associates and imitators, major and minor, and evolved into an art with many various disciplines and characteristics. From the beginning the Pre-Raphaelites were both popular and notorious, exciting both the scorn of such detractors as Charles Dickens and the spirited support of such defenders as John Ruskin. The Pre-Raphaelites were lampooned in the newspapers on the one hand, and invited to decorate the halls of the aristocracy on the other. The Pre-Raphaelite aesthetic influenced such disparate men as W. B. Yeats and G. B. Shaw, George Meredith and Gerard Manley Hopkins, D. H. Lawrence and Ezra Pound, as well as the artists of the Aesthetic Movement, Symbolism and Art Nouveau. Today, continuing exhibitions of Pre-Raphaelite painting, the proliferation of poster and greeting card reproductions of Pre-Raphealite art, such influenced modern works as John Fowles' excellent novel *The French Lieutenant's Woman* and of course the boom in fantasy literature indebted to Morris, are evidence that Pre-Raphaelitism has not passed from the earth. As Marcel Duchamp has said, the Pre-Raphaelites "lit a small flame which is still burning despite everything."

Pre-Raphaelite art is difficult to define, as variegated as it is, but there are certain characteristics of even the earliest paintings which generally anticipate the whole movement. The paintings of the original Brotherhood are of narrative subjects borrowed from literature, rendered with vivid color and meticulous detail work. In all its descendant forms, in poetry, prose and ornament, Pre-Raphaelite art remains literary in bias and highly wrought in technique. In its first and shortest phase, dominated by Hunt, Pre-Raphaelite paintings are often crowded with morally pointed symbolism. In its second phase, dominated by Rossetti, moralism gives way to escapism, and Pre-Raphaelitism becomes an otherwordly art of etherealized damozels and pallid knights in heavily brocaded medievalesque settings.

In the mid-fifties Rossetti, stung by criticism of his earliest paintings on religious subjects, withdrew from the moral activism of Hunt and began painting romantic figure subjects, more in keeping with his own emotional and poetic impulses. And together with a set of younger disciples, he became an enthusiastic participant in the contemporary Gothic revival.

Such men as Ruskin, Carlyle and Tennyson, following the lead of Walter Scott, were celebrating a romantic vision of the Middle Ages as a simpler, more noble time than that of modern England. But whereas the vision of these men was largely social in its bias, the Gothic vision of the Pre-Raphaelites was artistic and fantastic. The Middle Ages, Burne-Jones said, were "such stuff as dreams are made on." Especially it was Rossetti, an admirer and important popularizer of the Romantic poets Blake and Keats as well as the contemporary American writer Edgar Allan Poe, who crossed Gothicism with supernaturalism and formed an art which was mystic, wistful and weird.

Almost all of Victorian art is a second flowering of the Romantic art which preceded it, but the peculiarity of the Pre-Raphaelites is that unlike their fellow Victorians they were Romantics without shame. The nineteenth century was a new and perilous time. The Industrial Revolution was changing the way in which people lived, and Darwinian science was changing the way in which people believed. The Modern Age was being born and it was widely felt that art had a moral responsibility to adapt itself and be useful in difficult times. It was not a time for artistic introspection. The Romantic indulgence in private emotions could no longer be afforded in a time of public need.

Most Victorian artists, therefore, struggled to renounce the Romantic legacy. Carlyle and Arnold were outspokenly hostile to Romanticism ("a channel for thinking aloud, instead of making anything," Arnold complained), but their own brooding self-centered works give them away. J. S. Mill walked a rope, trying to reconcile his emotional admiration for Wordsworth with his intellectual commitment to utilitarian reform. Tennyson tried heroically to be a didactic poet, fitting his work for public use, but always his backward eye was fixed passionately upon the private "Palace of Art." Browning spent much of his career fighting a hopeless battle with the ghost of Shelley. Charlotte Brontë, after the death of her sisters, struggled to put away Byron and childish things and write novels that would instruct. Even Dickens managed to fix a frown on his face and climb into the pulpit.

The almost constant tension, between the self-absorbed inward looking which was the legacy of the Romantics and the public-spirited outward looking which was the challenge of the new age, produced much of what is great in Victorian art. The Pre-Raphaelites produced an art of different greatness by refusing to suffer the dilemma. The case of William Morris seems to present a singular exception, of course, for he devoted much of his life to social reform, and yet he spent his final years writing fantastic tales which have nothing to do with socialism and the commonweal. He once said, "I can't enter into politico-social subjects with any interest, for on the whole I see that things are in a muddle, and I have no power or vocation to set them right in ever so little a degree. My work is the embodiment of dreams in one form or another."

For the most part the Pre-Raphaelites suffered no difficulty in deciding between a former and the present age. Their path was a straight road leading to the past and they never looked back to the future. As Keats had often done they delved into the mythically medieval for their themes and they ornamented these with antique and archaic images. They ornamented so lavishly, in fact, that their pictures and poems and prose often lack compositional strength. Substance becomes subordinate to description and decoration, and emotional and sensual effects take the place of precise definitions of meaning. Like a medieval suit of armor, which may be splendid indeed but hollow as well, there is no center.

Unlike even the Romantics, who at least put their own bared souls at the center of their art, the Pre-Raphaelites developed a separatist art which is often neither introverted nor extroverted, fitted neither for private revelation nor public use. They pioneered a concept which was to shape the last generation of Victorian art and be carried to its extreme during the Aesthetic Movement of the century's end: Art for art's sake.

The artistic nature of the Pre-Raphaelites is evident in the following collection of their works of short fiction. The prose is opulent and dense, the images painted in with fine detail and many colors. The themes are taken from an unreal romance world of dark ladies and enchanted lovers, of strange illnesses and sudden deaths, of omens and miracles and mysteries. These are stories not of complex meaningfulness but of arresting and emotional beauty. They are stories of fantasy. They are embodiments of dreams.

Because of the multiple forms of Pre-Raphaelite art, it has been an inevitable feature of Pre-Raphaelite criticism (and appreciation) to regard poems of the Pre-Raphaelites in terms of their paintings, their paintings in terms of their poems, their paintings and poems in terms of their work in the decorative arts, and so forth. Now, for the first time, we have their collected short stories, and though short fiction is a minor element of the Pre-Raphaelite canon, this unique collection provides a new and valuable perspective from which to consider Pre-Raphaelite art and the nature and uses of the Pre-Raphaelite imagination.

A note on the text

The three stories by Swinburne were written between 1858 and 1860, when the young poet was attempting to write a cycle of prose tales in imitation of Boccaccio. The project, to be titled *The Triameron,* was abandoned, and only one of the stories, *Dead Love,* was published in his lifetime. All three appeared in the twenty-volume Bonchurch edition of his collected works, published 1925-1927.

Rossetti's *Hand and Soul* (1849) and *St. Agnes of Intercession* (1850) appeared in The Germ, the short-lived organ of the original Pre-Raphaelite Brotherhood. Both stories show the young Rossetti's attempts to define the role of the painter, in characteristically supernatural terms. The fatalistic but moving story *The Orchard Pit* is a much later work, written in 1869 not long before an unsuccessful suicide attempt. All three stories appeared in the two-volume collected works prepared by his brother, W. M. Rossetti, published in 1886.

The other stories in this collection appeared only in The Oxford and Cambridge Magazine, published monthly during 1856 by a group of Oxford students which included Morris and Burne-Jones as well as William Fulford and R. W. Dixon, both of whom were to take orders and become churchmen. The magazine, financed by Morris and edited by Fulford, was inspired by the Pre-Raphaelite Brotherhood's The Germ, and similarly contained poetry, essays and criticism as well as prose tales.

Most of the tales were by Morris and were of a fantastic nature which anticipated the long prose romances of his last years. The tales, like the prose romances, have been reprinted in various modern editions, widely available today, and so are not included in the present collection. The one Morris tale included here, which apparently has never been published independently of The Oxford and Cambridge Magazine, is not fantasy, but a splendidly romantic story of love lost. It exhibits presciently and therefore poignantly that aspect of Morris' psychology which so colored much of his great poetry as well as his last great romances, a sexual fatalism which his first biographer, J. W. Mackail, called a "singular and almost a morbid attraction, that of the unsuccessful man and despised lover."

Except for a very few editorial corrections, the stories in this collection appear exactly in their original forms.

—John Weeks

The Marriage of Mona Lisa

By Algernon Charles Swinburne

There was a certain maiden in Pisa who strangely loved a young man but he liked her little: nevertheless she was very fair, delicate and tall: her name was Mona Lisa. Now it came to pass that one sought her in marriage who was a rich man of good birth. Then the mother of this damsel spoke to her and said: "Thou seest now, Lisa, how we are altogether become poor and of little esteem; also my hands are soft to work, and thine eyes are futile. Now therefore it were but shame and no profit if we should turn to any labour: and if thou wed not this man, I shall doubtless die of pure sorrow." Then the maiden wept a great while, laying her face in the lap of her gown so that many tears fell down between her knees and on her little coloured shoes. At last she said, still weeping much : "O fair mother, the will of God is great and bitter, and pain is very strong to prevail with a woman, but a man shall overcome and cast out pain. Behold now, I will do after your word, and so if I die God shall deliver me out of all pain." Then she cried out once or twice as if some great anguish had bitten in her very flesh; and lay some while with her body all bowed and twisted. And in time she drew in her feet and put her arms about her knees and sighed sore: then she arose off her bed and went out and came to the house of the rich man. And he opened the doors: and when he beheld this damsel, he fell down only with joy, and kissed her on her feet. And she said: "Sir, I am come hither to be your wife, if you will." Thereat he cried out and praised God, and kissed her head and her lips. Then they went in together. And she said to him: "Sir, if God shall help me, I will always be to you a true good wife and live as a pure woman." And he beheld her in the face as one that was a little perplexed; but he saw she was so fair and chaste that her words had none but a clean meaning; and he was full glad and kissed her again. And she, looking sadly on him, said again: "Sir, if it please you, we will not wait long to be married." But she was so weak and sick with the great pain of heart inside her that she thought little of what she said but only how she might quickly be done with this pain. And for all things else she was most innocent, as one that was quite simple and pure. Which he understanding, as he was a noble man and courteous, and was aware of all things harmless and noble at sight of them, rejoiced only the more for her goodwill and made her the best cheer of heart and face that may be thought of. And then she returned home and told her mother: and her mother was very glad: and being an old woman and evil-minded, she imagined with herself that the maiden had some desire of goodwill towards the beauty and body of this knight, or else that she had some commerce with another, and was ashamed; but in all this matter she was very foolish and ignorant. And the little damsel knew none of these things. And it happened on the night before her marriage, that being very weary and having a heat and sickness in her body, she clothed herself poorly and went forth and came to the house of the man whom she loved with her whole heart: and there was a great feast made. And the noise of the music and of the singing women that danced and sang shamefully, striking full on her that stood outside, made her head beat and ache as if the bare sunlight burned upon it. And she bowed herself over a little wall of red bricks that was next the street, and wept very pitifully.

And in the house there was a violent noise and laughter of har-
lots. Now after the space of an hour, when she was tired of
weeping, she rose up to go away. But for pure pain only she
could not set her feet to go. And she fell down upon the stone
passage weeping, and kissed the doors; and her sweet and yellow
hair was defiled with dust and ravelled. And presently there
came one out of the house that trod upon part of her hair and
she cried out. Then this man took her in both hands and drew
her into the house and laid her down: then went and told his
master, saying "Sir, here is another of them." And he laughed,
and said, "Eh!" once or twice, as was his fashion when he was
pleased, and this man was very lascivious. So he went out, smiling in his beard, and came to the damsel. Then she said to him:
"Alas, sir, you know that for very many days I have loved you
with all the strength in my heart: and never in all my life have
you done me any little grace or had any pity upon me. Nevertheless, sir, God knows that in all this His great world there is not
anything made that is more miserable and sorrowful than I am.
This is now the sixth month that I have had no pleasure to live:
and if God have mercy upon me, as I believe He shall have
mercy, I shall not come into the seventh month. For I have wept
so much that all my blood is gone into bitter tears and wasted
with weeping out of my feeble body. And now, sir, I must in the
morning be married to a man who loves me full eagerly, and he
is a good man: and afterwards till I die I shall be his. Therefore I
pray of you that you will give me a kiss now." And when she had
said this she held up her mouth sorrowfully, as a child after he
has been well beaten, that he may be kissed for pity. Then he was
touched a little, and gave her the kiss: but he said nothing. And
thus they departed.

Now on the morrow the marriage was made very sumptu-
ously, and after the feast was begun the damsel went up alone to
her chamber. And she sat there beside the bed and beheld idly
this way and that way. And the maids and young men laughed
greatly and jested: and one that was a light woman began to
speak lewdly concerning her. Then the bridegroom was angry
and rose and went after her. And seeing him enter she looked
silently upon his face. And in her own face there was great sor-

row, but neither fear nor any shame whatever. Then he sat down and held her hands with his own, and they felt very heavy. And leaning over towards her he kissed her on the mouth lovingly, keeping hold of her hands. Then she sighed on a sudden and slipped sideways towards him, so that she sat on the floor with her head lying between his knees; and so died in a little while: whereof her husband made much sorrow, and she was buried with a great fame. Upon whose soul I believe assuredly that God had pity, because she died maiden and although she was very loving.

Dead Love

By Algernon Charles Swinburne

About the time of the great troubles in France, that fell out between the parties of Armagnac and of Burgundy, there was slain in a fight in Paris a follower of the Duke John, who was a good knight called Messire Jacques d'Aspremont. This Jacques was a very fair and strong man, hardy of his hands, and before he was slain he did many things wonderful and of great courage, and forty of the folk of the other party he slew, and many of these were great captains, of whom the chief and the worthiest was Messire Olivier de Bois-Percé; but at last he was shot in the neck with an arrow, so that between the nape and the apple the flesh was cleanly cloven in twain. And when he was dead his men drew forth his body of the fierce battle, and covered it with a fair woven cloak. Then the people of Armagnac, taking good heart because of his death, fell the more heavily upon his followers, and slew very many of them. And a certain soldier, named Amaury de Jacqueville, whom they called Courtebarbe, did best of all that party; for, crying out with a great noise, "Sus, sus!" he brought up the men after him, and threw them forward into the hot part of the fighting, where there was a sharp clamour; and this Amaury, laughing and crying out as a man that took a great delight in such matters of war, made of himself more noise with smiting and with shouting than any ten, and they of Burgundy were astonished and beaten down. And when he was weary, and his men had got the upper hand of those of Burgundy, he left off slaying, and beheld where Messire d'Aspremont was covered up with his cloak; and he lay just across the door of Messire Olivier, whom the said Jacques had slain, who was also a cousin of Amaury's. Then said Amaury:

"Take up now the body of this dead fellow, and carry it into the house; for my cousin Madame Yolande shall have great delight to behold the face of the fellow dead by whom her husband has got his end, and it shall make the tiding sweeter to her."

So they took up this dead knight Messire Jacques, and carried him into a fair chamber lighted with broad windows, and herein sat the wife of Olivier, who was called Yolande de Craon, and she was akin far off to Pierre de Craon, who would have slain the Constable. And Amaury said to her:

"Fair and dear cousin, and my good lady, we give you for your husband slain the body of him that slew my cousin; make the best cheer that you may, and comfort yourself that he has found a good death and a good friend to do justice on his slayer; for this man was a good knight, and I that have revenged him account myself none of the worst."

And with this Amaury and his people took leave of her. Then Yolande, being left alone, began at first to weep grievously, and so much that she was heavy and weary; and afterward she looked upon the face of Jacques d'Aspremont, and held one of his hands with hers, and said:

"Ah, false thief and coward! it is great pity thou wert not hung on a gallows, who hast slain by treachery the most noble knight of the world, and to me the most loving and the faithfullest man alive, and that never did any discourtesy to any man, and was the most single and pure lover that ever a married lady had to be her knight, and never said any word to me but sweet words. Ah, false coward! there was never such a knight of thy kin."

Then, considering his face earnestly, she saw that it was a fair face enough, and by seeming the face of a good knight; and she repented of her bitter words, saying with herself:

"Certainly this one, too, was a good man and valiant," and was sorry for his death.

And she pulled out the arrow-head that was broken, and closed up the wound of his neck with ointments. And then beholding his dead open eyes, she fell into a great torrent of weeping, so that her tears fell all over his face and throat. And all the time of this bitter sorrow she thought how goodly a man this Jacques must have been in his life, who being dead had such power upon her pity. And for compassion of his great beauty she wept so exceedingly and long that she fell down upon his body in a swoon, embracing him, and so lay the space of two hours with her face against his; and being awaked she had no other desire but only to behold him again, and so all that day neither ate nor slept at all, but for the most part lay and wept. And afterward, out of her love, she caused the body of this knight to be preserved with spice, and made him a golden coffin open at the top, and clothed him with the fairest clothes she could get, and had this coffin always by her bed in her chamber. And when this was done she sat down over against him and held his arms about her neck, weeping, and she said:

"Ah, Jacques! although alive I was not worthy, so that I never saw the beauty and goodness of your living body with my sorrowful eyes, yet now being dead, I thank God that I have this grace to behold you. Alas, Jacques! you have no right now to discern what things are beautiful, therefore you may now love me as well as another, for with dead men there is no difference of women. But, truly, although I were the fairest of all Christian women that now is, I were in nowise worthy to love you; nevertheless, have compassion upon me that for your sake have forgotten the most noble husband of the world."

And this Yolande, that made such complaining of love to a dead man, was one of the fairest ladies of all that time, and of great reputation; and there were many good men that loved her greatly, and would fain have had some favour at her hands; of whom she made no account, saying always, that her dead lover was better than many lovers living. Then certain people said that she was bewitched; and one of these was Amaury. And they would have taken the body to burn it, that the charm might be brought to an end; for they said that a demon had entered in and taken it in possession; which she hearing fell into extreme rage, and said that if her lover were alive, there was not so good a knight among them, that he should undertake the charge of that saying; at which speech of hers there was great laughter. And upon a night there came into her house Amaury and certain others, that were minded to see this matter for themselves. And no man kept the doors; for all her people had gone away, saving only a damsel that remained with her; and the doors stood open, as in a house where there is no man. And they stood in the doorway of her chamber, and heard her say this that ensues:—

"O most fair and perfect knight, the best that ever was in any time of battle, or in any company of ladies, and the most courteous man, have pity upon me, most sorrowful woman and handmaid. For in your life you had some other lady to love you, and were to her a most true and good lover; but now you have none other but me only, and I am not worthy that you should so much as kiss me on my sad lips, wherein is all this lamentation. And though your own lady were the fairer and the more worthy, yet consider, for God's pity and mine, how she has forgotten the love of your body and the kindness of your espousals, and loves easily with some other man, and is wedded to him with all honour; but I have neither ease nor honour, and yet I am your true maiden and servant."

And then she embraced and kissed him many times. And Amaury was very wroth, but he refrained himself: and his friends were troubled and full of wonder. Then they beheld how she held his body between her arms, and kissed him in the neck with all her strength; and after a certain time it seemed to them that the body of Jacques moved and sat up; and she was no whit amazed, but arose up with him, embracing him. And Jacques said to her:

"I beseech you, now that you would make a covenant with me, to love me always."

And she bowed her head suddenly, and said nothing.

Then said Jacques:

"Seeing you have done so much for love of me, we twain shall never go in sunder: and for this reason has God given back to me the life of my mortal body."

And after this they had the greatest joy together, and the most perfect solace that may be imagined: and she sat and beheld him, and many times fell into a little quick laughter for her great pleasure and delight.

Then came Amaury suddenly into the chamber, and caught his sword into his hand, and said to her:

"Ah, wicked leman, now at length is come the end of thy horrible love and of thy life at once"; and smote her through the two sides with his sword, so that she fell down, and with a great sigh full unwillingly delivered up her spirit, which was no sooner fled out of her perishing body, but immediately the soul departed also out of the body of her lover, and he became as one that had been all those days dead. And the next day the people caused their two bodies to be burned openly in the place where witches were used to be burned: and it is reported by some that an evil spirit was seen to come out of the mouth of Jacques d'Aspremont, with a most pitiful cry, like the cry of a hurt beast. By which thing all men knew that the soul of this woman, for the folly of her sinful and most strange affection, was thus evidently given over to the delusion of the evil one and the pains of condemnation.

The Portrait

By Algernon Charles Swinburne

There was a certain woman in the city of Pistoja who loved a man that was a painter; but she was espoused to one that was a merchant, and on a day she was married to him with great solemnity.

For many weeks this painter would come to her, and she would find means to withdraw herself from her husband that she might be the more given up to his love.

Now he, that is the painter, was a man of very evil conversation, and the woman became by his means infected with much wickedness; so that once she said to him: "Now, little Peter" (for thus she called him often, and his name was Messer Pietro Guastagni Bacafoli), "I would have you paint me a little picture which a man shall not look upon without loving, and so if he touch it he shall certainly die." But this painter laughed greatly and said: "How shall I then live if I paint it?" "Now," she said, "I shall show you, little Peter. Take a mask of glass, and also thick gloves on your hands, and work always till you can paint well without putting them off; and then paint me holding three roses, two red and a white between, to signify how I abide always between two men that love me, but the sweetness of either is not alike. And when this picture is finished you shall give it to my husband; and for love of me he will certainly give it a kiss or twain on its mouth; and when he is dead we will burn the picture."

Then this Peter greatly commended her, for he was a man that rejoiced in all manner of shameful dealing, and was also unclean of his life, as is the fashion of men that paint and men that make songs and verses; for this Peter also made many amorous poems, and played upon stringed instruments marvellously well. And the lives of such men as are painters, or such as are poets, are most often evil and foolish; therefore it may be well conceived of this Peter that he was a very lewd man.

Now in six weeks he had well-nigh finished this picture, and she sat to be painted in a little close gown of green sewn about with ornaments of gold, and the lining was of a tender and clouded colour between violet-blue and grey-blue. And all this the painter had painted very beautifully, for he put all his love and the strong lust of his evil will into the picture. Also he was used to paint the bodies of beautiful women that were naked, which is a very grievous thing in the opinion of God. And he had drawn her with her head a little stooped, as was her fashion for the weight of gold and heavy pearls that she wore above her hair, her husband being very rich, and also that she might show more fully the glorious turn of her throat; for it was very round and long, and wonderfully soft, for nothing was so delicate but the wearing of it would leave a mark in the tender flesh that was coloured like pearl colour. And in this wise was the painting done. She had her gown all ungirt on one side (I believe it was the left side) and the fastenings of it undone; so that all her body from the breast downward, and over against the flank, was naked between two edges of gold colour that met like two lips. And the beauty of her body was a great wonder. And one who saw this picture some way off says yet to this day that to behold it was like the hearing of strong music or the drinking of sweet wine; for not the wonder and hunger of the eyes only, but also the mouth and the ears were feasted and fully satisfied with the delicious-

ness of the painting of it; and to men beholding it it was as the
burning of a great perfume which they smelt.

Therefore it is certain that the sinful delight of one sense
draws after it, yea, plucks on as with a net, the delight which is in
the whole body of sin; and it is well not to have one sense open to
any sweet invasion of the abominable flesh wherein all sin abides
and increases as in fat ground. For out of earth is all our flesh
made, and earth is compounded of tears and sin, by reason
whereof it is always feeble and sorrowful even until it returns to
the unclean beginning. And when this grievous body of our enduring sin is wasted again into tears and dust, and the heaviness
of it is become light, and the holiness of it is become naked, then
the sinfulness of it does not pass into earth, neither is it used to
compound any other body; but it abides as a great and blind
beast that is tied with fetters and fast bound, and at the last it
shall be loosed and shall prey upon the soul as with sharp teeth.

And out of this death there shall be no afterbirth of redemp-
tion. And to the sad body there shall be no remission made, and
to the weary and heavy soul there shall be no ease given. For this
death, which begins upon the first and fleshly death, shall endure always and wax great, and increase when all things shall be
utterly abolished. Alas, now, what profit shall any man gather of
these unprofitable things? I beseech therefore of all beautiful
and gracious women and tender ladies, and lordly men that are
strong and cunning, that they take good heed of all this matter.
For the end of such sweet feeding is very bitter and pitiful.
Therefore shall many tears be wept out of eyes that wept never
yet, to behold the end of all this, for the end is most bitter. And in
the delicate and perfumed mouths that ate honey gladly, and
were filled between lip and lip with the strong kisses of love,
there shall be the taste of blood and sharp gall. And in the pleasant flesh shall be the burning of whips like as fire. And the eyes
shall flow over, and the blood become weak, and the loins of one
shall be bruised, and the sides of another shall be broken. And in
no side of the body shall there be any breath, neither any savour
of ease; but the body shall be thoroughly consumed.

Now in such a manner was this picture finished; and Messer
Gian having a good will to see it came to the house of this Peter.

And the lady sat over against them and played with a large cat; for both she and this aforesaid Peter loved such things much. Then said Messer Gian, "Might not one give this picture a kiss on its mouth?" And they laughed violently. Then he kissed it, and there was a bitter savour in his lips, and they smarted therewith. So he said, "Messer Pietro, this lady is not so sweet for one to kiss, but I shall find a means to take out this bitterness."

Alas the folly of this man! For he knew not that whereas St. Paul spake concerning the lust of the eye, he spake not only against the eye of a man, but also against his mouth and all his members, that all should be cleanly governed and washed in sweet water; and by the desire of his ignorant lips was this man destroyed.

Then afterwards he came to his wife, and kissed her suddenly. And she, feeling the savour of a violent death on his lips (for his mouth was not yet wiped), cried out and smote him on the said mouth. Then he marvelled, and she crying always out on him, and reviling him with the most grievous words in any way imaginable, besought the man that was her lover to fetch some medicine for her kissed mouth. Then her husband would fain have taken hold of her to embrace her. But she cried and wept the more exceedingly, saying she was poisoned. Then the said Peter took her between his arms sadly, and said in this wise, "Seeing now, my beloved lady, and all the comfort of my body, that your life by my deed is brought in certain peril of a bitter end, I am resolved that I will not behold the time of your burial with my weeping eyes, but after death will be your friend with all the love and little wisdom that is in me. Therefore have courage, for I shall bring it certainly to pass that all good lovers of ladies shall say prayers for our sake." So full of a shameless wit was this man, and thus sweetly could he make use of his intolerable sin; but undoubtedly God hath before this time confuted his foolishness with a very sharp reason.

Then Messer Gian was so wrath that he would presently have slain them, but for the might of the poison that waxed in him he could not pull forth his sword, and so cursed at them with a great rage, and presently died.

Then the lady, bitterly weeping and embracing her said lover with her hands and body, yet so as her lips should nowise touch him, also yielded up her spirit without any feintence, as one certainly delivered over to the shameful possession and government of her extreme love. Which things becoming presently known, the said picture was cut in twain and burned, and the painter of it taken and hanged in sight of a great multitude; and this was all the wages that this Peter had for his good painting. Certainly therefore it may be supposed that this manner of craft, except it be of a chaste habit, and only employed in the likeness of holy things, is without doubt very displeasing to God.

"And when this story was finished," says the Author of the original "Triameron," "they all laughed more exceedingly than before, for they understood well that Messer Vittore was a very good painter, and feared God little, being a loose-living man."

The Orchard Pit

By Dante Gabriel Rossetti

Men tell me that sleep has many dreams; but all my life I have dreamt one dream alone.

I see a glen whose sides slope upward from the deep bed of a dried-up stream, and either slope is covered with wild apple-trees. In the largest tree, within the fork whence the limbs divide, a fair, golden-haired woman stands and sings, with one white arm stretched along a branch of the tree, and with the other holding forth a bright red apple, as if to some one coming down the slope. Below her feet the trees grow more and more tangled, and stretch from both sides across the deep pit below: and the pit is full of the bodies of men.

They lie in heaps beneath the screen of boughs, with her apples bitten in their hands; and some are no more than ancient bones now, and some seem dead but yesterday. She stands over them in the glen, and sings for ever, and offers her apple still.

This dream shows me no strange place. I know the glen, and have known it from childhood, and heard many tales of those who have died there by the Siren's spell.

I pass there often now, and look at it as one might look at a place chosen for one's grave. I see nothing, but I know that it means death for me. The apple-trees are like others, and have childish memories connected with them, though I was taught to shun the place.

No man sees the woman but once, and then no other is near; and no man sees that man again.

One day, in hunting, my dogs tracked the deer to that dell, and he fled and crouched under that tree, but the dogs would not go near him. And when I approached, he looked in my eyes as if to say, "Here you shall die, and will you here give death?" And his eyes seemed the eyes of my soul, and I called off the dogs, who were glad to follow me, and we left the deer to fly.

I know that I must go there and hear the song and take the apple. I join with the young knights in their games; and have led our vassals and fought well. But all seems to be a dream, except what only I among them all shall see. Yet who knows? Is there one among them doomed like myself, and who is silent, like me? We shall not meet in the dell, for each man goes there alone: but in the pit we shall meet each other, and perhaps know.

Each man who is the Siren's choice dreams the same dream, and always of some familiar spot wherever he lives in the world, and it is there that he finds her when his time comes. But when he sinks in the pit, it is the whole pomp of her dead gathered through the world that awaits him there; for all attend her to grace her triumph. Have they any souls out of those bodies? Or are the bodies still the house of the soul, the Siren's prey till the day of judgment?

We were ten brothers. One is gone there already. One day we looked for his return from a border foray, and his men came home without him, saying that he had told them he went to seek his love who would come to meet him by another road. But anon his love met them, asking for him; and they sought him vainly all that day. But in the night his love rose from a dream; and she went to the edge of the Siren's dell, and there lay his helmet and his sword. And her they sought in the morning, and there she lay dead. None has ever told this thing to my love, my sweet love who is affianced to me.

One day at table my love offered me an apple. And as I took it she laughed, and said, "Do not eat, it is the fruit of the Siren's dell." And I laughed and ate: and at the heart of the apple was a red stain like a woman's mouth; and as I bit it I could feel a kiss upon my lips.

The same evening I walked with my love by that place, and she would needs have me sit with her under the apple-tree in which the Siren is said to stand. Then she stood in the hollow fork of the tree, and plucked an apple, and stretched it to me and would have sung: but at that moment she cried out, and leaped from the tree into my arms, and said that the leaves were whispering other words to her, and my name among them. She threw the apple to the bottom of the dell, and followed it with her eyes, to see how far it would fall, till it was hidden by the tangled boughs. And as we still looked, a little snake crept up through them.

She would needs go with me afterwards to pray in the church, where my ancestors and hers are buried; and she looked round on the effigies, and said, "How long will it be before we lie here carved together?" And I thought I heard the wind in the apple-trees that seemed to whisper, "How long?"

And late that night, when all were asleep, I went back to the dell, and said in my turn, "How long?" And for a moment I seemed to see a hand and apple stretched from the middle of the tree where my love had stood. And then it was gone: and I plucked the apples and bit them, and cast them in the pit, and said, "Come."

I speak of my love, and she loves me well; but I love her only as the stone whirling down the rapids loves the dead leaf that travels with it and clings to it, and that the same eddy will swallow up.

Last night, at last, I dreamed how the end will come and now I know it is near. I not only saw, in sleep, the lifelong pageant of the glen, but I took my part in it at last, and learned for certain why that dream was mine.

I seemed to be walking with my love among the hills that lead downward to the glen: and still she said, "It is late;" but the wind was glenwards, and said, "Hither." And still she said, "Home grows far;" but the rooks flew glenwards, and said, "Hither." And still she said, "Come back;" but the sun had set, and the moon laboured towards the glen, and said, "Hither." And my heart said in me, "Aye, thither at last." Then we stood on the margin of the slope, with the apple-trees beneath us; and the moon bade the clouds fall from her and sat in her throne like the sun at noon-day: and none of the apple-trees were bare now, though autumn was far worn, but fruit and blossom covered them together. And they were too thick to see through clearly; but looking far down I saw a white hand holding forth an apple, and heard the first notes of the Siren's song. Then my love clung to me and wept; but I began to struggle down the slope through the thick wall of bough and fruit and blossom, scattering them as the storm scatters the dead leaves; for that one apple only would my heart have. And my love snatched at me as I went; but the branches I thrust away sprang back on my path, and tore her hands and face: and the last I knew of her was the lifting of her hands to heaven as she cried aloud above me, while I still forced my way downwards. And now the Siren's song rose clearer as I went. At first she sang, "Come to Love;" and of the sweetness of Love she said many things. And next she sang, "Come to Life;" and Life was sweet in her song. But long before I reached her, she knew that all her will was mine: and then her voice rose softer than ever, and her words were, "Come to Death;" and Death's name in her mouth was the very swoon of all sweetest things that be. And then my path cleared; and she stood over against me in the fork of the tree I knew so well, blazing now like a lamp beneath the moon. And one kiss I had of her mouth, as I took the apple from her hand. But while I bit it, my brain whirled and my foot stumbled; and I felt my crashing fall through the tangled boughs beneath her feet, and saw the dead white faces that welcomed me in the pit. And so I woke cold in my bed: but it still seemed that I lay indeed at last among those who shall be my mates for ever, and could feel the apple still in my hand.

Saint Agnes of Intercession

By Dante Gabriel Rossetti

Among my earliest recollections, none is stronger than that of my father standing before the fire when he came home in the London winter evenings, and singing to us in his sweet, generous tones: sometimes ancient English ditties,—such songs as one might translate from the birds, and the brooks might set to music; sometimes those with which foreign travel had familiarized his youth,—among them the great tunes which have rung the world's changes since '89. I used to sit on the hearth-rug, listening to him, and look between his knees into the fire till it burned my face, while the sights swarming up in it seemed changed and changed with the music: till the music and the fire and my heart burned together, and I would take paper and pencil, and try in some childish way to fix the shapes that rose within me. For my hope, even then, was to be a painter.

The first book I remember to have read, of my own accord, was an old-fashioned work on Art, which my mother had, —

Hamilton's "English Conoscente." It was a kind of continental tour,—sufficiently Della-Cruscan, from what I can recall of it,—and contained notices of pictures which the author had seen abroad, with engravings after some of them. These were in the English fashion of that day, executed in stipple and printed with red ink; tasteless enough, no doubt, but I yearned towards them and would toil over them for days. One especially possessed for me a strong and indefinable charm: it was a Saint Agnes in glory, by Bucciolo d'Orli Angiolieri. This plate I could copy from the first with much more success than I could any of the others; indeed, it was mainly my love of the figure, and a desire to obtain some knowledge regarding it, which impelled me, by one magnanimous effort upon the "Conoscente," to master in a few days more of the difficult art of reading than my mother's laborious inculcations had accomplished till then. However, what I managed to spell and puzzle out related chiefly to the executive qualities of the picture, which could be little understood by a mere child; of the artist himself, or the meaning of his work, the author of the book appeared to know scarcely anything.

As I became older, my boyish impulse towards art grew into a vital passion; till at last my father took me from school and permitted me my own bent of study. There is no need that I should dwell much upon the next few years of my life. The beginnings of Art, entered on at all seriously, present an alternation of extremes:—on the one hand, the most bewildering phases of mental endeavour, on the other, a toil rigidly exact and dealing often with trifles. What was then the precise shape of the cloud within my tabernacle, I could scarcely say now; or whether through so thick a veil I could be sure of its presence there at all. And as to which statue at the Museum I drew most or learned least from,—or which Professor at the Academy "set" the model in the worst taste,—these are things which no one need care to know. I may say, briefly, that I was wayward enough in the pursuit, if not in the purpose; that I cared even too little for what could be taught me by others; and that my original designs greatly outnumbered my school-drawings.

In most cases where study (such study, at least, as involves any practical elements) has benumbed that subtle transition which brings youth out of boyhood, there comes a point, after some time, when the mind loses its suppleness and is riveted merely by the continuance of the mechanical effort. It is then that the constrained senses gradually assume their utmost tension, and any urgent impression from without will suffice to scatter the charm. The student looks up: the film of their own fixedness drops at once from before his eyes, and for the first time he sees his life in the face.

In my nineteenth year, I might say that, between one path of Art and another, I worked hard. One afternoon I was returning, after an unprofitable morning, from a class which I attended. The day was one of those oppressive lulls in autumn, when application, unless under sustained excitement, is all but impossible,—when the perceptions seem curdled and the brain full of sand. On ascending the stairs to my room, I heard voices there, and when I entered, found my sister Catharine, with another young lady, busily turning over my sketches and papers, as if in search of something. Catharine laughed, and introduced her companion as Miss Mary Arden. There might have been a little malice in the laugh, for I remembered to have heard the lady's name before, and to have then made in fun some teasing inquiries about her, as one will of one's sisters' friends. I bowed for the introduction, and stood rebuked. She had her back to the window, and I could not well see her features at the moment; but I made sure she was very beautiful, from her tranquil body and the way that she held her hands. Catharine told me they had been looking together for a book of hers which I had had by me for some time, and which she had promised to Miss Arden. I joined in the search, the book was found, and soon after they left my room. I had come in utterly spiritless; but now I fell to and worked well for several hours. In the evening, Miss Arden remained with our family circle till rather late: till she left I did not return to my room, nor, when there, was my work resumed that night. I had thought her more beautiful than at first.

After that, every time I saw her, her beauty seemed to grow on my sight by gazing, as the stars do in water. It was some time before I ceased to think of her beauty alone; and even then it was still of her that I thought. For about a year my studies somewhat lost their hold upon me, and when that year was upon its close, she and I were promised in marriage.

Miss Arden's station in life, though not lofty, was one of more ease than my own, but the earnestness of her attachment to me had deterred her parents from placing any obstacles in the way of our union. All the more, therefore, did I now long to obtain at once such a position as should secure me from reproaching myself with any sacrifice made by her for my sake: and I now set to work with all the energy of which I was capable, upon a picture of some labour, involving various aspects of study. The subject was a modern one, and indeed it has often seemed to me that all work, to be truly worthy, should be wrought out of the age itself, as well as out of the soul of its producer, which must needs be a soul of the age. At this picture I laboured constantly and unweariedly, my days and my nights; and Mary sat to me for the principal female figure. The exhibition to which I sent it opened a few weeks before the completion of my twenty-first year.

Naturally enough, I was there on the opening day. My picture, I knew, had been accepted, but I was ignorant of a matter perhaps still more important,—its situation on the walls. On that now depended its success; on its success the fulfilment of my most cherished hopes might almost be said to depend. That is not the least curious feature of life as evolved in society,—which, where the average strength and the average mind are equal, as in this world, becomes to each life another name for destiny,— when a man, having endured labour, gives its fruit into the hands of other men, that they may do their work between him and mankind: confiding it to them, unknown, without seeking knowledge of them; to them, who have probably done in like wise before him, without appeal to the sympathy of kindred experience: submitting to them his naked soul, himself, blind and unseen: and with no thought of retaliation, when, it may be, by their judgment, more than one year, from his dubious three-score and ten, drops alongside, unprofitable, leaving its baffled labour for its successors to recommence. There is perhaps no proof more complete how sluggish and little arrogant, in aggregate life, is the sense of individuality.

I dare say something like this may have been passing in my

mind as I entered the lobby of the exhibition, though the princi-
ple, with me as with others, was subservient to its application; my
thoughts, in fact, starting from and tending towards myself and
my own picture. The kind of uncertainty in which I then was is
rather a nervous affair; and when, as I shouldered my way
through the press, I heard my name spoken close behind me, I
believe that I could have wished the speaker further off without
being particular as to distance. I could not well, however, do
otherwise than look round, and on doing so, recognized in him
who had addressed me a gentleman to whom I had been introduced overnight at the house of a friend, and to whose remarks
on the Corn question and the National Debt I had listened with a
wish for deliverance somewhat akin to that which I now felt; the
more so, perhaps, that my distaste was coupled with surprise; his
name having been for some time familiar to me as that of a
writer of poetry.

As soon as we were rid of the crush, we spoke and shook
hands; and I said, to conceal my chagrin, some platitudes as to
Poetry being present to support her sister Art in the hour of trial.

"Oh just so, thank you," said he; "have you anything here?"

While he spoke, it suddenly struck me that my friend, the
night before, had informed me this gentleman was a critic as well
as a poet. And indeed, for the hippopotamus-fronted man, with
his splay limbs and wading gait, it seemed the more congenial
vocation of the two. In a moment, the instinctive antagonism
wedged itself between the artist and the reviewer, and I avoided
his question.

He had taken my arm, and we were now in the gallery together. My companion's scrutiny was limited almost entirely to
the "line," but my own glance wandered furtively among the
suburbs and outskirts of the ceiling, as a misgiving possessed me
that I might have a personal interest in those unenviable "high
places" of art. Works, which at another time would have absorbed my whole attention, could now obtain from me but a
restless and hurried examination: still I dared not institute an
open search for my own, lest thereby I should reveal to my companion its presence in some dismal condemned corner which
might otherwise escape his notice. Had I procured my catalogue,

I might at least have known in which room to look, but I had omitted to do so, thinking thereby to know my fate the sooner, and never anticipating so vexatious an obstacle to my search. Meanwhile I must answer his questions, listen to his criticism, observe and discuss. After nearly an hour of this work, we were not through the first room. My thoughts were already bewildered, and my face burning with excitement.

By the time we reached the second room, the crowd was more dense than ever, and the heat more and more oppressive. A glance round the walls could reveal but little of the consecrated "line," before all parts of which the backs were clustered more or less thickly; except, perhaps, where at intervals hung the work of some venerable member, whose glory was departed from him. The seats in the middle of the room were, for the most part, empty as yet: here and there only an unenthusiastic lady had been left by her party, and sat in stately unruffled toilet, her eye ranging apathetically over the upper portion of the walls, where the gilt frames were packed together in desolate parade. Over these my gaze also passed uneasily, but without encountering the object of its solicitude.

In this room my friend the critic came upon a picture, conspicuously hung, which interested him prodigiously, and on which he seemed determined to have my opinion. It was one of those tender and tearful works, those "labours of love," since familiar to all print-shop *flâneurs*,—in which the wax doll is made to occupy a position in Art which it can never have contemplated in the days of its humble origin. The silks heaved and swayed in front of this picture the whole day long.

All that we could do was to stand behind, and catch a glimpse of it now and then, through the whispering bonnets, whose "curtains" brushed our faces continually. I hardly knew what to say, but my companion was lavish of his admiration, and began to give symptoms of the gushings of the poet-soul. It appeared that he had already seen the picture in the studio, and being but little satisfied with my monosyllables, was at great pains to convince me. While he chattered, I trembled with rage and impatience.

"You must be tired," said he at last; "so am I; let us rest a little."

He led the way to a seat. I was his slave, bound hand and foot: I followed him.

The crisis now proceeded rapidly. When seated, he took from his pocket some papers, one of which he handed to me. Who does not know the dainty action of a poet fingering MS? The knowledge forms a portion of those wondrous instincts implanted in us for self-preservation. I was past resistance, however, and took the paper submissively.

"They are some verses," he said, "suggested by the picture you have just seen. I mean to print them in our next number, as being the only species of criticism adequate to such a work."

I read the poem twice over, for after the first reading I found I had not attended to a word of it, and was ashamed to give it him back. The repetition was not, however, much more successful, as regarded comprehension,—a fact which I have since believed (having seen it again) may have been dependent upon other causes besides my distracted thoughts. The poem, now included among the works of its author, runs as follows:—

> O thou who are not as I am,
>   Yet knowest all that I must be,—
>   O thou who livest certainly
> Full of deep meekness like a lamb
> Close laid for warmth under its dam,
>   On pastures bare towards the sea:—
>
> Look on me, for my soul is bleak,
>   Nor owns its labour in the years,
>   Because of the deep pain of tears:
> It hath not found and will not seek,
> Lest that indeed remain to speak
>   Which, passing, it believes it hears.
>
> Like ranks in calm unipotence
>   Swayed past, compact and regular,
>   Time's purposes and portents are:
> Yet the soul sleeps, while in the sense
> The graven brows of Consequence
>   Lie sunk, as in blind wells the star.

O gaze along the wind-strewn path
    That curves distinct upon the road
    To the dim purple-hushed abode.
Lo! autumntide and aftermath!
Remember that the year has wrath
    If the ungarnered wheat corrode.

It is not that the fears are sore
    Or that the evil pride repels:
    But there where the heart's knowledge dwells
The heart is gnawed within the core,
Nor loves the perfume from that shore
    Faint with bloom-pulvered asphodels.

Having atoned for non-attention by a second perusal, whose only result was non-comprehension, I thought I had done my duty towards this performance, which I accordingly folded up and returned to its author. He asked, in so many words, my opinion of it.

"I think," replied I coolly, "that when a poet strikes out for himself a new path in style, he should first be quite convinced that it possesses sufficient advantages to counterbalance the contempt which the swarm of his imitators will bring upon poetry."

My ambiguity was successful. I could see him take the compliment to himself, and inhale it like a scent, while a slow broad smile covered his face. It was much as if, at some meeting, on a speech being made complimentary to the chairman, one of the waiters should elbow that personage aside, plant his knuckles on the table, and proceed to return thanks.

And indeed, I believe my gentleman was about to do so in due form, but my thoughts, which had been unable to resist some enjoyment of his conceit, now suddenly reverted to their one dominant theme; and rising at once, in an indignant spleen at being thus harassed and beset, I declared that I must leave him, and hurry through the rest of the gallery by myself, for that I had an impending appointment. He rose also. As we were shaking hands, a part of the "line" opposite to where we stood was left bare by a lapse in the crowd. "There seems to be an odd-looking picture," said my companion. I looked in the same direction: the press was closing again; I caught only a glimpse of the canvas, but that sufficed: it was my own picture, *on the line!* For a moment, my head swam with me.

He walked towards the place, and I followed him. I did not at first hear well what he said of the picture; but when I did, I found he was abusing it. He called it quaint, crude, even grotesque; and certainly the uncompromising adherence to nature as then present before me, which I had attempted throughout, gave it, in the exhibition, a more curious and unique appearance than I could have anticipated. Of course only a very few minutes elapsed before my companion turned to the catalogue for the artist's name.

"They thought the thing good," he drawled as he ran his eye down the pages, "or it wouldn't be on the line. 605, 606, — or else the fellow has interest somewhere. 630, what the deuce am I thinking of? — 613, 613, 613 — Here it is — Why," he exclaimed, short of breath with astonishment, "the picture is yours!"

"Well, it seems so," said I, looking over his shoulder; "I suppose they're likely to know."

"And so you wanted to get away before we came to it. And so the picture is yours!"

"Likely to remain so too," I replied laughing, "if every one thinks as well of it as you do."

"Oh! mind you," he exclaimed, "you must not be offended: one always finds fault first: I am sure to congratulate you."

The surprise he was in made him speak rather loud, so that people were beginning to nudge each other, and whisper that I was the painter. I therefore repeated hurriedly that I really must go, or I should miss my appointment.

"Stay a minute," ejaculated my friend the critic; "I am trying to think what the style of your picture is like. It is like the works of a very early man that I saw in Italy. Angioloni, Angellini, *Angiolieri*, that was the name, Bucciuolo Angiolieri. He always turned the toes in. The head of your woman there" (and he pointed to the figure painted from Mary) "is exactly like a St. Agnes of his at Bologna."

A flash seemed to strike before my eyes as he spoke. The name mentioned was a part of my first recollection; and the picture he spoke of. . . . Yes, indeed, there, in the face of my betrothed bride, I beheld the once familiar features of the St. Agnes, forgotten since childhood! I gazed fixedly on the work of my own hands; and thought turned in my brain like a wheel.

When I looked again towards my companion, I could see that he was wondering at my evident abstraction. I did not explain, but abruptly bidding him good-bye, hastened out of the exhibition.

As I walked homewards, the cloud was still about me, and the street seemed to pass me like a shadow. My life had been, as it were, drawn by, and the child and the man brought together. How had I not at once recognized, in her I loved, the dream of my childhood? Yet, doubtless, the sympathy of relation, though unconscious, must have had its influence. The fact of the likeness was a mere casualty, however singular; but that which had cast the shadow of the man's love in the path of the child, and left the seed at his heart to work its growth blindly in darkness, was surely much more than chance.

Immediately on reaching home, I made inquiries of my mother concerning my old friend the "English Conoscente"; but learned, to my disappointment, that she had long since missed the book, and had never recovered it. I felt vexed in the extreme.

The joy with which the news of my picture was hailed at home may readily be imagined. There was one, however, to whom it may have been more welcome even than to my own household: to her, as to myself, it was hope seen nearer. I could scarcely have assigned a reason why I refrained from mentioning to her, or to any one, the strange point of resemblance which I had been led to perceive; but from some unaccountable reluctance I kept it to myself at the time. The matter was detailed in the journal of the worthy poet-critic who had made the discovery; such scraps of research being much too scarce not to be worked to their utmost; it may be too that my precipitate retreat had left him in the belief of my being a convicted plagiarist. I do not think, however, that either Mary's family or my own saw the paper; and indeed it was much too aesthetic to permit itself many readers.

Meanwhile, my picture was obtaining that amount of notice, favourable with unfavourable, which constitutes success, and was not long in finding a purchaser. My way seemed clearing before me. Still, I could not prevent my mind from dwelling on the curious incident connected with the painting, and which, by constant brooding upon it, had begun to assume, in my idea, almost the character of a mystery. The coincidence was the more singular that my work, being in subject, costume, and accessories, English, and of the present period, could scarcely have been expected to suggest so striking an affinity in style to the productions of one of the earliest Italian painters.

The gentleman who purchased my picture had commissioned me at the same time for another. I had always entertained a great wish to visit Italy, but now a still stronger impulse than before drew me thither. All substantial record having been lost, I could hardly persuade myself that the idol of my childhood, and the worship I had rendered it, was not all an unreal dream: and every day the longing possessed me more strongly to look with my own eyes upon the veritable St. Agnes. Not holding myself free to marry as yet, I therefore determined (having it now within my power) that I would seek Italy at once, and remain there while I painted my next picture. Nor could even the thought of leaving Mary deter me from this resolution.

On the day I quitted England, Mary's father again placed her hand in mine, and renewed his promise; but our own hearts were a covenant between us.

From this point, my narrative will proceed more rapidly to its issue. Some lives of men are as the sea is, continually vexed and trampled with winds. Others are, as it were, left on the beach. There the wave is long in reaching its tide-mark, where it abides but a moment; afterwards, for the rest of that day, the water is shifted back more or less slowly; the sand it has filled hardens; and hourly the wind drives lower till nightfall.

To dwell here on my travels any further than in so much as they concern the thread of my story, would be superfluous. The first place where I established myself, on arriving in the Papal State, was Bologna, since it was there, as I well remembered, that the St. Agnes of Bucciuolo Angiolieri was said to be. I soon became convinced, however, after ransacking the galleries and private collections, that I had been misinformed. The great Clementine is for the most part a dismal wilderness of Bolognese Art, "where nothing is that hath life," being rendered only the more ghastly by the "life-in-death" of Guido and the Caracci; and the private collectors seem to emulate the Clementine.

From Bologna I removed to Rome, where I stayed only for a month, and proceeded thence into Tuscany. Here, in the painter's native province, after all, I thought the picture was most likely to be found; as is generally the case with artists who have produced comparatively few works, and whose fame is not of the highest order of all. Having visited Siena and Arezzo, I took up my abode in Florence. Here, however, seeing the necessity of getting to work at once, I commenced my next picture, devoting to it a certain number of hours each day; the rest of my time being chiefly spent among the galleries, where I continued my search. The St. Agnes still eluded me; but in the Pitti and elsewhere, I met with several works of Bucciuolo; in all of which I thought, in fact, that I could myself recognize, despite the wide difference both of subject and occasional treatment, a certain mental approximation, not easily defined, to the style of my own productions. The peculiarities of feeling and manner which had attracted my boyish admiration had evidently sunk deep, and maintained, though hitherto unperceived, their influence over me.

I had been at Florence for about three months, and my picture was progressing, though slowly enough; moreover, the other idea which engrossed me was losing its energy, by the recurrence of defeat, so that I now determined on leaving the thing mainly to chance, and went here and there, during the hours when I was not at work, seeing what was to see. One day, however, being in a bookseller's shop, I came upon some numbers of a new Dictionary of Works of Art, then in course of publication, where it was stated that a painting of St. Agnes, by Bucciuolo Angiolieri, was in the possession of the Academy of Perugia. This then, doubtless, was the work I wished to see; and when in the Roman States, I must already have passed upon my search through the town which contained it. In how many books had I rummaged for the information which chance had at length thrown in my way! I was almost inclined to be provoked with so inglorious a success. All my interest in the pursuit, however, revived at once, and I immediately commenced taking measures for retracing my steps to Perugia. Before doing so I despatched a long letter to Mary, with whom I kept up a correspondence, telling her where to direct her next missive, but without informing her as to the motive of my abrupt removal, although in my letter I dwelt at some length, among other topics, on those works of Bucciuolo which I had met with at Florence.

I arrived at Perugia late in the evening, and to see the gallery before the next morning was out of the question. I passed a most restless night. The same one thought had been more or less with me during the whole of my journey, and would not leave me now until my wish was satisfied. The next day proved to be one on which the pictures were not visible; so that on hastening to the Academy in the morning, I was again disappointed. Upon the second day, had they refused me admittance, I believe I should have resorted to desperate measures. The doors however were at last wide open. Having put the swarm of guides to rout, I set my feet on the threshold; and such is the power of one absorbing idea, long suffered to dwell on the mind, that as I entered I felt my heart choke me as if with some vague apprehension.

This portion of my story which the reader has already gone through is so unromantic and easy of belief, that I fear the startling circumstances which remain to be told will jar upon him all the more by contrast as a clumsy fabrication. My course, however, must be to speak on, relating to the best of my memory things in which the memory is not likely to have failed; and reserving at least my own inward knowledge that all the events of this narrative (however unequal the measure of credit they may obtain) have been equally, with myself, matters of personal experience.

The Academy of Perugia is, in its little sphere, one of the high places of privilege; and the first room, the Council Chamber, full of rickety arm chairs, is hung with the presentation pictures of the members, a collection of indigenous grandeurs of the school of David. I purchased a catalogue of an old woman who was knitting in one corner, and proceeded to turn the leaves with nervous anxiety. Having found that the Florentine pictures were in the last room, I commenced hurrying across the rest of the gallery as fast as the polish of the waxed boards would permit. There was no visitor besides myself in the rooms, which were full of Roman, Bolognese, and Perugian handiwork: one or two students only, who had set up their easels before some masterpiece of the "advanced" style, stared round in wonder at my irreverent haste. As I walked, I contined my search in the catalogue; so that, by the time I reached the Florentine room, I had found the number, and walked, with a beating heart, straight up to the picture.

The picture is about half the size of life; it represents a beautiful woman, seated, in the costume of the painter's time, richly adorned with jewels; she holds a palm branch, and a lamb nestles to her feet. The glory round her head is a device pricked without colour on the gold background, which is full of the faces of angels. The countenance was the one known to me, by a feeble reflex, in childhood; it was also the exact portrait of Mary, feature by feature. I had been absent from her for more than five months, and it was like seeing her again.

As I looked, my whole life seemed to crowd about me, and to stun me like a pulse in my head. For some time I stood lost in astonishment, admiration, perplexity helpless of conjecture, and an almost painful sense of love.

I had seen that in the catalogue there was some account of the picture; and now, after a long while, I removed my eyes, dizzy with gazing and with thought, from the face, and read in Italian as follows:

"*No. 212. St. Agnes, with a glory of angels. By Bucciuolo Angiolieri.*

"Bertuccio, Buccio or Bucciuolo d'Orlí Angiolieri, a native of Cignana in the Florentine territory, was born in 1405 and died in 1460. He was the friend, and has been described as the pupil, of Benozzo Gozzoli; which latter statement is not likely to be correct, since their ages were nearly the same, as are also the dates of their earliest known pictures.

"He is said by some to have been the first to introduce a perfectly nude figure in a devotional subject (the St. Sebastian now at Florence); an opinion which Professor Ehrenhaupt has called in question, by fixing the date of the five anonymous frescoes in the Church of Sant' Andrea d'Oltr 'arno, which contain several nude figures, at a period antecedent to that in which he flourished. His works are to be met with at Florence, at Lucca, and in one or two cities of Germany. The present picture, though ostensibly representing St. Agnes, is the portrait of Blanzifiore dall 'Ambra, a lady to whom the painter was deeply attached, and who died early. The circumstances connected by tradition with the painting of this picture are of a peculiarly melancholy nature.

"It appears that, in the vicissitudes of faction, the lady's family were exiled from Florence, and took refuge at Lucca; where some of them were delivered by treachery to their enemies and put to death. These accumulated misfortunes (not the least among which was the separation from her lover, who, on account of his own ties and connections, could not quit Florence), preyed fatally on the mind and health of Blanzifiore; and before many months had passed, she was declared to be beyond medicinal aid. No sooner did she learn this, than her first thought was of the misery which her death would occasion her lover; and she insisted on his being summoned immediately from Florence, that they might at least see each other once again upon earth. When, on his arrival, she witnessed his anguish at thus losing her for ever, Blanzifiore declared that she would rise at once from her bed, and that Bucciuolo should paint her portrait before she died; for so, she said, there should still remain something to him whereby to have her in memory. In this will she persisted against all remonstrance occasioned by the fears of her friends; and for two days, though in a dying state, she sat with wonderful energy to her lover: clad in her most sumptuous attire, and arrayed with all her jewels: her two sisters remaining constantly at her side, to sustain her and supply restoratives. On the third day, while Bucciuolo was still at work, she died without moving.

"After her death, Bucciuolo finished the portrait, and added to it the attributes of St. Agnes, in honour of her purity. He kept it always near him during his lifetime; and, in dying, bequeathed it to the Church of Santa Agnese dei Lavoranti, where he was buried at her side. During all the years of his life, after the death of Blanzifiore, he remained at Lucca: where some of his works are still to be found.

"The present picture has been copied many times, but never competently engraved; and was among those conveyed to Paris by Bonaparte, in the days of his omnipotence."

The feeling of wonder which attained bewilderment, as I proceeded with this notice, was yet less strong than an intense penetrating sympathy excited in me by the unhappy narrative, which I could not easily have accounted for, but which so overcame me that, as I finished, the tears stung my eyes. I remained for some time leaning upon the bar which separated me from the picture, till at last my mind settled to more definite thought. But thought here only served to confound. A woman had then lived four hundred years since, of whom that picture was the portrait; and my own eyes bore me witness that it was also the surpassingly perfect resemblance of a woman now living and breathing,—of my own affianced bride! While I stood, these things grew and grew upon my mind, till my thoughts seemed to hustle about me like pent-up air.

The catalogue was still open in my hand; and now, as my eyes wandered, in aimless distraction, over the page, they were arrested by these words: *"No. 231. Portrait of Bucciuolo Angiolieri painted by himself."* At first my bewildered perceptions scarcely attached a meaning to the words; yet, owing no doubt to the direction of my thoughts, my eye dwelt upon them, and continued to peruse them over and over, until at last their purport flashed upon me. At the same instant that it did so, I turned round and glanced rapidly over the walls for the number: it was at the other end of the room. A trembling suspense, with something almost of involuntary awe, was upon me as I ran towards the spot; the picture was hung low; I stooped over the rail to look closely at it, and was face to face with *myself!* I can recall my feeling at that moment, only as one of the most lively and exquisite fear.

It was myself, of nearly the same age as mine was then, but perhaps a little older. The hair and beard were of my colour,

trimmed in an antique fashion; and the dress belonged to the
early part of the fifteenth century. In the background was a portion of the city of Florence. One of the upper corners contained
this inscription:—

ALBERTUS ORLITIS ANGELERIUS
Ipsum ipse
ÆTAT. SUÆ XXIV.

That it *was* my portrait,—that the St. Agnes was the portrait of
Mary,—and that both had been painted by myself four hundred
years ago,—this now rose up distinctly before me as the one and
only solution of so startling a mystery, and as being, in fact, that
result round which, or some portion of which, my soul had been
blindly hovering, uncertain of itself. The tremendous experience
of that moment, the like of which has never, perhaps, been
known to any other man, must remain undescribed; since the
description, read calmly at common leisure, could seem but fantastic raving. I was as one who, coming after a wilderness to some
city dead since the first world, should find among the tombs a
human body in his own exact image, embalmed; having the
blackened coin still within its lips, and the jars still at its side, in
honour of gods whose very names are abolished.

After the first incapable pause, during which I stood rooted to
the spot, I could no longer endure to look on the picture, and
turning away, fled back through the rooms and into the street. I
reached it with the sweat springing on my forehead, and my face
felt pale and cold in the sun.

As I hurried homewards, amid all the chaos of my ideas, I had
clearly resolved on one thing,—namely, that I would leave
Perugia that night on my return to England. I had passports
which would carry me as far as the confines of Italy; and when
there I counted on somehow getting them signed at once by the
requisite authorities, so as to pursue my journey without delay.

On entering my room in the hotel where I had put up, I found
a letter from Mary lying on the table. I was too much agitated
with conflicting thoughts to open it at once; and therefore allowed it to remain till my perturbation should in some measure

have subsided. I drew the blinds before my windows, and covered my face to think; my forehead was still damp between my hands. At least an hour must have elapsed in that tumult of the spirit which leaves no impression behind, before I opened the letter.

It was an answer to the one which I had posted before leaving Florence. After many questions and much news of home, there was a paragraph which ran thus:—

"The account you give me of the works of Bucciuolo Angiolieri interested me greatly. I am surprised never to have heard you mention him before, as he appears to find so much favour with you. But perhaps he was unknown to you till now. How I wish I could stand by your side before his pictures, to enjoy them with you and hear you interpret their beauties! I assure you that what you say about them is so vivid, and shows so much insight into all the meanings of the painter, that, while reading, I could scarcely divest myself of the impression that you were describing some of your own works."

As I finished the last sentence, the paper fell from my hands. A solemn passage of scripture had been running in my mind; and as I again lay back and hid my now burning and fevered face, I repeated it aloud:—"How unsearchable are Thy judgments, and Thy ways past finding out!"

As I have said, my intention was to set out from Perugia that same night; but on making enquiry, I found that it would be impossible to do so before the morning, as there was no conveyance till then. Posthorses, indeed, I might have had, but of this my resources would not permit me to think. That was a troubled and gloomy evening for me. I wrote, as well as my disturbed state would allow me, a short letter to my mother, and one to Mary, to apprise them of my return; after which, I went early to bed, and, contrary to my expectations, was soon asleep.

That night I had a dream, which has remained as clear and whole in my memory as the events of the day: and so strange were those events—so apart from the rest of my life till then,— that I could sometimes almost persuade myself that my dream of that night also was not without a mystic reality.

I dreamt that I was in London, at the exhibition where my

picture had been; but in the place of my picture, which I could not see, there hung the St. Agnes of Perugia. A crowd was before it; and I heard several say that it was against the rules to hang that picture, for that the painter (naming me) was dead. At this, a woman who was there began to weep: I looked at her and perceived it to be Mary. She had her arm in that of a man who appeared to wear a masquerade dress; his back was towards me, and he was busily writing on some tablets; but on peering over his shoulder, I saw that his pencil left no mark where it passed, which he did not seem to perceive, however, going on as before. I spoke to Mary, but she continued crying and did not look up. I then touched her companion on the shoulder; but finding that he paid no attention, I shook him and told him to resign that lady's arm to me, as she was my bride. He then turned round suddenly, and showed me my own face with the hair and beard quaintly cut, as in the portrait of Bucciuolo. After looking mournfully at me, he said, "Not mine, friend, but neither thine:" and while he spoke, his face fell in like a dead face. Meantime, every one seemed pale and uneasy, and they began to whisper in knots; and all at once I found opposite me the critic I met at the gallery, who was saying something I could not understand, but so fast that he panted and kept wiping his forehead. Then my dream changed. I was going up stairs to my room at home, where I thought Mary was waiting to sit for her portrait. The staircase was quite dark; and as I went up, the voices of several persons I knew passed by me, as if they were descending; and sometimes my own among them. I had reached the top, and was feeling for the handle of the door, when it was opened suddenly by an angel; and looking in, I saw, not Mary, but a woman whose face was hidden with white light, and who had a lamb beside her that was bleating aloud. She knelt in the middle of the room, and I heard her say several times: "O Lord, it is more than he can bear. Spare him, O Lord, for her sake whom he consecrated to me." After this, music came out of heaven, and I thought to have heard speech; but instead, there was silence that woke me.

This dream must have occurred repeatedly in the course of the night, for I remember waking up in perfect darkness, overpowered with fear, and crying out in the words which I had heard spoken by the woman; and when I woke in the morning, it was from the same dream, and the same words were on my lips.

During the two days passed at Perugia, I had not had time to think of the picture I was engaged upon, which had therefore remained in its packing-case, as had also the rest of my baggage. I was thus in readiness to start without further preliminaries. My mind was so confused and disturbed that I have but a faint recollection of that morning; to the agitating events of the previous day, my dream had now added, in spite of myself, a vague foreboding of calamity.

No obstacle occurred throughout the course of my journey, which was, even at that recent date, a longer one than it is now. The whole time, with me, was occupied by one haunting and despotic idea: it accompanied me all day on the road; and if we paused at night it either held me awake or drove all rest from my sleep. It is owing to this, I suppose, that the wretched mode of conveyance, the evil roads, the evil weather, the evil inns, the harassings of petty authorities, and all those annoyances which are set as close as milestones all over the Continent, remain in my memory only with a general sense of discomfort. Moreover, on the day when I left Perugia I had felt the seeds of fever already in my veins; and during the journey this oppression kept constantly on the increase. I was obliged, however, carefully to conceal it, since the panic of the cholera was again in Europe, and any sign of illness would have caused me to be left at once on the road.

By the night of my arrival in London, I felt that I was truly and seriously ill; and, indeed, during the last part of the journey, physical suffering had for the first time succeeded in partially distracting my thought from the thing which possessed it. The first inquiries I made of my family were regarding Mary. I learned that she at least was still in good health, and anxiously looking for my arrival; that she would have been there, indeed, but that I had not been expected till a day later. This was a weight taken from my heart. After scarcely more than an hour passed among my family, I repaired to my bed; both body and mind had at length a perfect craving for rest. My mother, immediately on my arrival, had noticed my flushed and haggard appearance; but when questioned by her I attributed this to the fatigues of travelling.

In spite of my extreme need of sleep, and the wish I felt for it, I believe that I slept but little that night. I am not certain, however, for I can only remember that as soon as I lay down my head began to whirl till I seemed to be lifted out of my bed; but whether this were in waking or a part of some distempered dream, I cannot determine. This, however, is the last thing I can recall. The next morning I was in a raging fever, which lasted for five weeks.

Health and consciousness came back to me by degrees, as light and air towards the outlet of a long vault. At length, one day, I sat up in bed for the first time. My head felt light in the pillows; and the sunshine that warmed the room made my blood creep refreshingly. My father and mother were both with me.

As sense had deserted my mind, so had it returned, in the form of one constant thought. But this was now grown peremptory, absolute, uncompromising, and seemed to cry within me for speech, till silence became a torment. To-day, therefore, feeling for the first time, since my gradual recovery, enough of strength for the effort, I resolved that I would at last tell the whole to my parents. Having first warned them of the extraordinary nature of the disclosure I was about to make, I accordingly began. Before I had gone far with my story, however, my mother fell back in her seat, sobbing violently; then rose, and running up to me, kissed me many times, still sobbing and calling me her poor boy. She then left the room. I looked towards my father, and saw that he had turned away his face. In a few moments he rose also without looking at me, and went out as my mother had done.

I could not quite account for this, but was so weary of doubt and conjecture, that I was content to attribute it to the feelings excited by my narration and the pity of all those troubles which the events I spoke of had brought upon me. It may appear strange, but I believe it to have been the fact, that the startling and portentous reality which those events had for me, while it left me fully prepared for wonder and perturbation on the part of my hearers, prevented the idea from even occurring to me that, as far as belief went, there could be more hesitation in another's than in my own.

It was not long before my father returned. On my questioning him as to the cause of my mother's excitement, he made no explicit answer, but begged to hear the remainder of what I had to disclose. I went on, therefore, and told my tale to the end. When I had finished, my father again appeared deeply affected; but soon recovering himself, endeavoured, by reasoning, to persuade me either that the circumstances I had described had no foundation save in my own diseased fancy, or else that at the time of their occurrence incipient illness had caused me to magnify very ordinary events into marvels and omens.

Finding that I still persisted in my conviction of their actuality, he then informed me that the matters I had related were already known to himself and to my mother through the disjointed ravings of my long delirium, in which I had dwelt on the same theme incessantly; and that their grief, which I had remarked, was occasioned by hearing me discourse thus connectedly on the same wild and unreal subject, after they had hoped me to be on the road to recovery. To convince me that this could merely be the effect of prolonged illness, he led me to remark that I had never till then alluded to the topic, either by word or in any of my letters, although, by my account, the chain of coincidences had already begun before I left England. Lastly, he implored me most earnestly at once to resist and dispel this fantastic brainsickness, lest the same idea, allowed to retain possession of my mind, might end,—as he dreaded to think that it indeed might,—by endangering my reason.

My father's last words struck me like a stone in the mouth; there was no longer any answer that I could make. I was very weak at the time, and I believe I lay down in my bed and sobbed. I remember it was on that day that it seemed to me of no use to see Mary again, or, indeed, to strive again after any aim I had had, and that for the first time I wished to die; and then it was that there came distinctly, such as it may never have come to any other man, the unutterable suspicion of the vanity of death.

From that day until I was able to leave my bed, I never in any way alluded to the same terrible subject; but I feared my father's eye as though I had been indeed a madman. It is a wonder that I did not really lose my senses. I lived in a continual panic lest I should again speak of that matter unconsciously, and used to repeat inwardly, for hours together, words enjoining myself to silence. Several friends of the family, who had made constant inquiries during my illness, now wished to see me; but this I strictly refused, being in fear that my incubus might get the better of me, and that I might suddenly implore them to say if they had any recollection of a former existence. Even a voice or a whistle from the street would set me wondering whether that man had lived before, and if so, why I alone should be cursed with this awful knowledge. It was useless even to seek relief in books; for the name of any historical character occurring at once disturbed my fevered mind with conjectures as to what name its possessor *now* bore, who he was, and in what country his lot was cast.

For another week after that day I was confined to my room, and then at last I might go forth. Latterly, I had scarcely spoken to any one, but I do not think that either my father or my mother imagined I had forgotten. It was on a Sunday that I left the house for the first time. Some person must have been buried at the neighbouring church very early that morning, for I recollect that the first thing I heard upon waking was the funeral bell. I had had, during the night, but a restless throbbing kind of sleep; and I suppose it was my excited nerves which made me wait with a feeling of ominous dread through the long pauses of the tolling, unbroken as they were by any sound from the silent Sunday streets, except the twitter of birds about the housetops. The last knell had long ceased, and I had been lying for some time in bitter reverie, when the bells began to ring for church. I cannot express the sudden refreshing joy which filled me at that moment. I rose from my bed, and kneeling down, prayed while the sound lasted.

On joining my parents at breakfast, I made my mother repeat to me once more how many times Mary had called during my illness, and all that she had said and done. They told me that she would probably be there that morning; but my impatience would not permit me to wait; I must go and seek her myself at once. Often already, said my parents, she had wished and begged to see me, but they had feared for my strength. This was in my thoughts as I left the house; and when, shutting the door behind me, I stood once again in the living sunshine, it seemed as if her love burst around me like music.

I set out hastily in the well-known direction of Mary's house. While I walked through the crowded streets, the sense of reality grew upon me at every step, and for the first time during some months I felt a man among men. Any artist or thoughtful man whatsoever, whose life has passed in a large city, can scarcely fail, in course of time, to have some association connecting each spot continually passed and repassed with the labours of his own mind. In the woods and fields every place has its proper spell and mystery, and needs no consecration from thought; but wherever in the daily walk through the thronged and jarring city, the soul has read some knowledge from life, or laboured towards some birth within its own silence, there abides the glory of that hour, and the cloud rests there before an unseen tabernacle. And thus now, with myself, old trains of thought and the conceptions of former years came back as I passed from one swarming resort to another, and seemed, by contrast, to wake my spirit from its wild and fantastic broodings to a consciousness of something like actual existence; as the mere reflections of objects, sunk in the vague pathless water, appear almost to strengthen it into substance.

Hand and Soul

By Dante Gabriel Rossetti

Before any knowledge of painting was brought to Florence, there were already painters in Lucca, and Pisa, and Arezzo, who feared God and loved the art. The workmen from Greece, whose trade it was to sell their own works in Italy and teach Italians to imitate them, had already found in rivals of the soil a skill that could forestall their lessons and cheapen their labors, more years than is supposed before the art came at all into Florence. The pre-eminence to which Cimabue was raised at once by his contemporaries, and which he still retains to a wide extent even in the modern mind, is to be accounted for, partly by the circumstances under which he arose, and partly by that extraordinary *purpose of fortune* born with the lives of some few, and through which it is not a little thing for any who went before, if they are even remembered as the shadows of the coming of such an one, and the voices which prepared his way in the wilderness. It is thus, almost exclusively, that the painters of whom I speak are now known. They have left little, and but little heed is taken of that which men hold to have been surpassed; it is gone like time gone,—a track of dust and dead leaves that merely led to the fountain.

Nevertheless, of very late years and in very rare instances, some signs of a better understanding have become manifest. A case in point is that of the triptych and two cruciform pictures at Dresden, by Chiaro di Messer Bello dell' Erma, to which the eloquent pamphlet of Dr. Aemmster has at length succeeded in attracting the students. There is another still more solemn and beautiful work, now proved to be by the same hand, in the Pitti Gallery at Florence. It is the one to which my narrative will relate.

This Chiaro dell' Erma was a young man of very honourable family in Arezzo; where, conceiving art almost for himself, and loving it deeply, he endeavoured from early boyhood towards the imitation of any objects offered in nature. The extreme longing after a visible embodiment of his thoughts strengthened as his years increased, more even than his sinews or the blood of his life; until he would feel faint in sunsets and at the sight of stately persons. When he had lived nineteen years, he heard of the famous Giunta Pisano; and, feeling much of admiration, with perhaps a little of that envy which youth always feels until it has learned to measure success by time and opportunity, he determined that he would seek out Giunta, and, if possible, become his pupil.

Having arrived in Pisa, he clothed himself in humble apparel, being unwilling that any other thing than the desire he had for knowledge should be his plea with the great painter; and then, leaving his baggage at a house of entertainment, he took his way along the street, asking whom he met for the lodging of Giunta. It soon chanced that one of the city, conceiving him to be a stranger and poor, took him into his house and refreshed him; afterwards directing him on his way.

When he was brought to speech of Giunta, he said merely that he was a student, and that nothing in the world was so much at his heart as to become that which he had heard told of him with whom he was speaking. He was received with courtesy and consideration, and soon stood among the works of the famous artist.

But the forms he saw there were lifeless and incomplete; and a sudden exultation possessed him as he said within himself, "I am the master of this man." The blood came at first into his face, but the next moment he was quite pale and fell to trembling. He was able, however, to conceal his emotion; speaking very little to Giunta, but when he took his leave, thanking him respectfully.

After this, Chiaro's first resolve was, that he would work out thoroughly some one of his thoughts, and let the world know him. But the lesson which he had now learned, of how small a greatness might win fame, and how little there was to strive against, served to make him torpid, and rendered his exertions less continual. Also Pisa was a larger and more luxurious city than Arezzo; and when, in his walks, he saw the great gardens laid out for pleasure, and the beautiful women who passed to and fro, and heard the music that was in the groves of the city at evening, he was taken with wonder that he had never claimed his share of the inheritance of those years in which his youth was cast. And women loved Chiaro; for, in despite of the burthen of study, he was well-favoured and very manly in his walking; and, seeing his face in front, there was a glory upon it, as upon the face of one who feels a light round his hair.

So he put thought from him, and partook of his life. But, one night, being in a certain company of ladies, a gentleman that was there with him began to speak of the paintings of a youth named Bonaventura, which he had seen in Lucca; adding that Giunta Pisano might now look for a rival. When Chiaro heard this, the lamps shook before him and the music beat in his ears. He rose up, alleging a sudden sickness, and went out of that house with his teeth set. And, being again within his room, he wrote up over the door the name of Bonaventura, that it might stop him when he would go out.

He now took to work diligently, not returning to Arezzo, but remaining in Pisa, that no day more might be lost; only living entirely to himself. Sometimes, after nightfall, he would walk abroad in the most solitary places he could find; hardly feeling the ground under him, because of the thoughts of the day which held him in fever.

The lodging Chiaro had chosen was in a house that looked

upon gardens fast by the Church of San Petronio. It was here, and at this time, that he painted the Dresden pictures; as also, in all likelihood, the one—inferior in merit, but certainly his—which is now at Munich. For the most part he was calm and regular in his manner of study; though often he would remain at work through the whole of a day, not resting once so long as the light lasted; flushed, and with the hair from his face. Or, at times, when he could not paint, he would sit for hours in thought of all the greatness the world had known from of old; until he was weak with yearning, like one who gazes upon a path of stars.

He continued in this patient endeavour for about three years, at the end of which his name was spoken throughout all Tuscany. As his fame waxed, he began to be employed, besides easel-pictures, upon wall-paintings; but I believe that no traces remain to us of any of these latter. He is said to have painted in the Duomo; and D'Agincourt mentions having seen some portions of a picture by him which originally had its place above the high altar in the Church of the Certosa; but which, at the time he saw it, being very dilapidated, had been hewn out of the wall, and was preserved in the stores of the convent. Before the period of Dr. Aemmster's researches, however, it had been entirely destroyed.

Chiaro was now famous. It was for the race of fame that he had girded up his loins; and he had not paused until fame was reached; yet now, in taking breath, he found that the weight was still at his heart. The years of his labour had fallen from him, and his life was still in its first painful desire.

With all that Chiaro had done during these three years, and even before with the studies of his early youth, there had always been a feeling of worship and service. It was the peace-offering that he made to God and to his own soul for the eager selfishness of his aim. There was earth, indeed, upon the hem of his raiment; but *this* was of the heaven, heavenly. He had seasons when he could endure to think of no other feature of his hope than this. Sometimes it had even seemed to him to behold that day when his mistress—his mystical lady (now hardly in her ninth year, but whose smile at meeting had already lighted on his soul)—even she, his own gracious Italian Art—should pass, through the sun that never sets, into the shadow of the tree of life, and be seen of God and found good: and then it had seemed to him that he, with many who, since his coming, had joined the band of whom he was one (for, in his dream, the body he had worn on earth had been dead an hundred years), were permitted to gather round the blessed maiden, and to worship with her through all ages and ages of ages, saying, Holy, holy, holy. This thing he had seen with the eyes of his spirit; and in this thing had trusted, believing that it would surely come to pass.

But now, (being at length led to inquire closely into himself) even as, in the pursuit of fame, the unrest abiding after attainment had proved to him that he had misinterpreted the craving of his own spirit—so also, now that he would willingly have fallen back on devotion, he became aware that much of that reverence which he had mistaken for faith had been no more than the worship of beauty. Therefore, after certain days passed in perplexity, Chiaro said within himself, "My life and my will are yet before me: I will take another aim to my life."

From that moment Chiaro set a watch on his soul, and put his hand to no other works but only to such as had for their end the presentment of some moral greatness that should influence the beholder: and to this end, he multiplied abstractions, and forgot the beauty and passion of the world. So the people ceased to throng about his pictures as heretofore; and, when they were carried through town and town to their destination, they were no longer delayed by the crowds eager to gaze and admire; and no prayers or offerings were brought to them on their path, as to his Madonnas, and his Saints, and his Holy Children, wrought for the sake of the life he saw in the faces that he loved. Only the critical audience remained to him; and these, in default of more worthy matter, would have turned their scrutiny on a puppet or a mantle. Meanwhile, he had no more of fever upon him; but was calm and pale each day in all that he did and in his goings in and out. The works he produced at this time have perished—in all likelihood, not unjustly. It is said (and we may easily believe it), that, though more laboured than his former pictures, they were cold and unemphatic; bearing marked out upon them the measure of that boundary to which they were made to conform.

And the weight was still close at Chiaro's heart: but he held in his breath, never resting (for he was afraid), and would not know it.

Now it happened, within these days, that there fell a great feast in Pisa, for holy matters: and each man left his occupation; and all the guilds and companies of the city were got together for games and rejoicings. And there were scarcely any that stayed in the houses, except ladies who lay or sat along their balconies between open windows which let the breeze beat through the rooms and over the spread tables from end to end. And the golden cloths that their arms lay upon drew all eyes upward to see their beauty; and the day was long; and every hour of the day was bright with the sun.

So Chiaro's model, when he awoke that morning on the hot pavement of the Piazza Nunziata, and saw the hurry of people that passed him, got up and went along with them; and Chiaro waited for him in vain.

For the whole of that morning, the music was in Chiaro's room from the Church close at hand; and he could hear the sounds that the crowd made in the streets; hushed only at long intervals while the processions for the feast-day chanted in going under his windows. Also, more than once, there was a high clamour from the meeting of factious persons: for the ladies of both leagues were looking down; and he who encountered his enemy could not choose but draw upon him. Chiaro waited a long time idle; and then knew that his model was gone elsewhere. When at his work, he was blind and deaf to all else; but he feared sloth: for then his stealthy thoughts would begin to beat round and round him, seeking a point for attack. He now rose, therefore, and went to the window. It was within a short space of noon; and underneath him a throng of people was coming out through the porch of San Petronio.

The two greatest houses of the feud in Pisa had filled the church for that mass. The first to leave had been the Gherghiotti; who, stopping on the threshold, had fallen back in ranks along each side of the archway: so that now, in passing outward, the Marotoli had to walk between two files of men whom they hated, and whose fathers had hated theirs. All the chiefs were there and their whole adherents; and each knew the name of each. Every man of the Marotoli, as he came forth and saw his foes, laid back his hood and gazed about him, to show the badge upon the close cap that held his hair. And of the Gherghiotti there were some who tightened their girdles; and some shrilled and threw up their wrists scornfully, as who flies a falcon; for that was the crest of their house.

On the walls within the entry were a number of tall narrow pictures, presenting a moral allegory of Peace, which Chiaro had painted that year for the Church. The Gherghiotti stood with their backs to these frescoes; and among them Golzo Ninuccio, the youngest noble of the faction, called by the people Golaghiotta, for his debased life. This youth had remained for some while talking listlessly to his fellows, though with his sleepy sunken eyes fixed on them who passed: but now, seeing that no man jostled another, he drew the long silver shoe off his foot and struck the dust out of it on the cloak of him who was going by, asking him how far the tides rose at Viderza. And he said so because it was three months since, at that place, the Gherghiotti had beaten the Marotoli to the sands, and held them there while the sea came in; whereby many had been drowned. And, when he had spoken, at once the whole archway was dazzling with the light of confused swords; and they who had left turned back; and they who were still behind made haste to come forth; and there was so much blood cast up the walls on a sudden, that it ran in long streams down Chiaro's paintings.

Chiaro turned himself from the window; for the light felt dry between his lids, and he could not look. He sat down, and heard the noise of contention driven out of the church-porch and a great way through the streets; and soon there was a deep murmur that heaved and waxed from the other side of the city, where those of both parties were gathering to join in the tumult.

Chiaro sat with his face in his open hands. Once again he had wished to set his foot on a place that looked green and fertile; and once again it seemed to him that the thin rank mask was about to spread away, and that this time the chill of the water must leave leprosy in his flesh. The light still swam in his head, and bewildered him at first; but when he knew his thoughts, they were these:—

"Fame failed me: faith failed me: and now this also,—the hope that I nourished in this my generation of men,—shall pass from me, and leave my feet and my hands groping. Yet because of this are my feet become slow and my hands thin. I am as one who, through the whole night, holding his way diligently, hath smitten the steel unto the flint, to lead some whom he knew darkling; who hath kept his eyes always on the sparks that himself made, lest they should fail; and who, towards dawn, turning to bid them that he had guided God speed, sees the wet grass untrodden except of his own feet. I am as the last hour of the day, whose chimes are a perfect number; whom the next followeth not, nor light ensueth from him; but in the same darkness is the old order begun afresh. Men say, 'This is not God nor man; he is not as we are, neither above us: let him sit beneath us, for we are many.' Where I write Peace, in that spot is the drawing of swords, and there men's footprints are red. When I would sow, another harvest is ripe. Nay, it is much worse with me than thus much. Am I not as a cloth drawn before the light, that the looker may not be blinded? but which sheweth thereby the grain of its own coarseness, so that the light seems defiled, and men say, 'We will not walk by it.' Wherefore through me they shall be doubly accursed, seeing that through me they reject the light. May one be a devil and not know it?"

As Chiaro was in these thoughts, the fever encroached slowly on his veins, till he could sit no longer and would have risen; but suddenly he found awe within him, and held his head bowed, without stirring. The warmth of the air was not shaken; but there seemed a pulse in the light, and a living freshness, like rain. The silence was a painful music, that made the blood ache in his temples; and he lifted his face and his deep eyes.

A woman was present in his room, clad to the hands and feet with a green and grey raiment, fashioned to that time. It seemed that the first thoughts he had ever known were given him as at first from her eyes, and he knew her hair to be the golden veil through which he beheld his dreams. Though her hands were joined, her face was not lifted, but set forward; and though the gaze was austere, yet her mouth was supreme in gentleness. And as he looked, Chiaro's spirit appeared abashed of its own intimate presence, and his lips shook with the thrill of tears; it seemed such a bitter while till the spirit might be indeed alone.

She did not move closer towards him, but he felt her to be as much with him as his breath. He was like one who, scaling a great steepness, hears his own voice echoed in some place much higher than he can see, and the name of which is not known to him. As the woman stood, her speech was with Chiaro: not, as it were, from her mouth or in his ears; but distinctly between them.

"I am an image, Chiaro, of thine own soul within thee. See me, and know me as I am. Thou sayest that fame has failed thee, and faith failed thee; but because at least thou hast not laid thy life unto riches, therefore, though thus late, I am suffered to come into thy knowledge. Fame sufficed not, for that thou didst seek fame: seek thine own conscience (not thy mind's conscience, but thine heart's), and all shall approve and suffice. For Fame, in noble soils, is a fruit of the Spring: but not therefore should it be said: 'Lo! my garden that I planted is barren: the crocus is here, but the lily is dead in the dry ground, and shall not lift the earth that covers it: therefore I will fling my garden together, and give it unto the builders.' Take heed rather that thou trouble not the wise secret earth; for in the mould that thou throwest up shall the first tender growth lie to waste; which else had been made strong in its season. Yea, and even if the year fall past in all its months, and the soil be indeed, to thee, peevish and incapable, and though thou indeed gather all thy harvest, and it suffice for others, and thou remain vexed with emptiness; and others drink of thy streams, and the drouth rasp thy throat;—let it be enough that these have found the feast good, and thanked the giver: remembering that, when the winter is striven through, there is another year, whose wind is meek, and whose sun fulfilleth all."

While he heard, Chiaro went slowly on his knees. It was not to her that spoke, for the speech seemed within him and his own. The air brooded in sunshine, and though the turmoil was great outside, the air within was at peace. But when he looked in her eyes, he wept. And she came to him, and cast her hair over him, and took her hands about his forehead, and spoke again:—

"Thou hast said," she continued, gently, "that faith failed thee. This cannot be. Either thou hadst it not, or thou hast it. But who bade thee strike the point betwixt love and faith? Wouldst thou sift the warm breeze from the sun that quickens it? Who bade thee turn upon God and say: 'Behold, my offering is of earth, and not worthy: Thy fire comes not upon it; therefore, though I slay not my brother whom Thou acceptest, I will depart before Thou smite me.' Why shouldst thou rise up and tell God He is not content? Had He, of His warrant, certified so to thee? Be not nice to seek out division; but possess thy love in sufficiency: assuredly this is faith, for the heart must believe first. What He hath set in thine heart to do, that do thou; and even though thou do it without thought of Him, it shall be well done; it is this sacrifice that He asketh of thee, and His flame is upon it for a sign. Think not of Him; but of His love and thy love. For God is no morbid exactor: He hath no hand to bow beneath, nor a foot, that thou shouldst kiss it."

And Chiaro held silence, and wept into her hair which covered his face; and the salt tears that he shed ran through her hair upon his lips; and he tasted the bitterness of shame.

Then the fair woman, that was his soul, spoke again to him saying:

"And for this thy last purpose, and for those unprofitable truths of thy teaching,—thine heart hath already put them away, and it needs not that I lay my bidding upon thee. How is it that thou, a man, wouldst say coldly to the mind what God hath said to the heart warmly? Thy will was honest and wholesome; but look well lest this also be folly,—to say, 'I, in doing this, do strengthen God among men.' When at any time hath He cried unto thee, saying, 'My son, lend Me thy shoulder, for I fall'? Deemest thou that the men who enter God's temple in malice, to the provoking of blood, and neither for His love nor for His wrath will abate their purpose,—shall afterwards stand, with thee in the porch midway between Him and themselves, to give ear unto thy thin voice, which merely the fall of their visors can drown, and to see thy hands, stretched feebly, tremble among their swords? Give thou to God no more than He asketh of thee;

but to man also, that which is man's. In all that thou doest, work from thine own heart, simply; for his heart is as thine, when thine is wise and humble; and he shall have understanding of thee. One drop of rain is as another, and the sun's prism in all: and shalt thou not be as he, whose lives are the breath of One? Only by making thyself his equal can he learn to hold communion with thee, and at last own thee above him. Not till thou lean over the water shalt thou see thine image therein: stand erect, and it shall slope from thy feet and be lost. Know that there is but this means whereby thou mayst serve God with man:—Set thine hand and thy soul to serve man with God."

And when she that spoke had said these words within Chiaro's spirit, she left his side quietly, and stood up as he had first seen her: with her fingers laid together, and her eyes steadfast, and with the breadth of her long dress covering her feet on the floor. And, speaking again, she said:—

"Chiaro, servant of God, take now thine Art unto thee, and paint me thus, as I am, to know me: weak, as I am, and in the weeds of this time; only with eyes which seek out labour, and with a faith, not learned, yet jealous of prayer. Do this; so shall thy soul stand before thee always, and perplex thee no more."

And Chiaro did as she bade him. While he worked, his face grew solemn with knowledge: and before the shadows had turned, his work was done. Having finished, he lay back where he sat, and was asleep immediately: for the growth of that strong sunset was heavy about him, and he felt weak and haggard; like one just come out of a dusk, hollow country, bewildered with echoes, where he had lost himself, and who has not slept for many days and nights. And when she saw him lie back, the beautiful woman came to him, and sat at his head, gazing, and quieted his sleep with her voice.

The tumult of the factions had endured all that day through all Pisa, though Chiaro had not heard it: and the last service of that feast was a mass sung at midnight from the windows of all the churches for the many dead who lay about the city, and who had to be buried before morning, because of the extreme heats.

———

In the spring of 1847, I was at Florence. Such as were there at the same time with myself—those, at least, to whom Art is something,—will certainly recollect how many rooms of the Pitti Gallery were closed through that season, in order that some of the pictures they contained might be examined and repaired without the necessity of removal. The hall, the staircases, and the vast central suite of apartments, were the only accessible portions; and in these such paintings as they could admit from the sealed *penetralia* were profanely huddled together, without respect of dates, schools, or persons.

I fear that, through this interdict, I may have missed seeing many of the best pictures. I do not mean *only* the most talked of: for these, as they were restored, generally found their way somehow into the open rooms, owing to the clamours raised by the students; and I remember how old Ercoli's, the curator's, spectacles used to be mirrored in the reclaimed surface, as he leaned mysteriously over these works with some of the visitors, to scrutinize and elucidate.

One picture that I saw that spring, I shall not easily forget. It was among those, I believe, brought from the other rooms, and had been hung, obviously out of all chronology, immediately beneath that head by Raphael so long known as the *Berrettino*, and now said to be the portrait of Cecco Ciulli.

The picture I speak of is a small one, and represents merely the figure of a woman, clad to the hands and feet with a green and grey raiment, chaste and early in its fashion, but exceedingly simple. She is standing: her hands are held together lightly, and her eyes set earnestly open.

The face and hands in this picture, though wrought with great delicacy, have the appearance of being painted at once, in a single sitting: the drapery is unfinished. As soon as I saw the figure, it drew an awe upon me, like water in shadow. I shall not attempt to describe it more than I have already done; for the most absorbing wonder of it was its literality. You knew that figure, when painted, had been seen; yet it was not a thing to be seen of men. This language will appear ridiculous to such as have never looked on the work; and it may be even to some among those who have. On examining it closely, I perceived in one corner of the canvas the words *Manus Animam pinxit,* and the date 1239.

I turned to my catalogue, but that was useless, for the pictures were all displaced. I then stepped up to the Cavaliere Ercoli, who was in the room at the moment, and asked him regarding the subject and authorship of the painting. He treated the matter, I thought, somewhat slightingly, and said that he could show me the reference in the catalogue, which he had compiled. This, when found, was not of much value, as it merely said, "Schizzo d'autore incerto," adding the inscription. I could willingly have prolonged my inquiry, in the hope that it might somehow lead to some result; but I had disturbed the curator from certain yards of Guido, and he was not communicative. I went back, therefore, and stood before the picture till it grew dusk.

The next day I was there again; but this time a circle of students was round the spot, all copying the *Berrettino.* I contrived, however, to find a place whence I could see *my* picture, and where I seemed to be in nobody's way. For some minutes I remained undisturbed; and then I heard, in an English voice: "Might I beg of you, sir, to stand a little more to this side, as you interrupt my view."

I felt vexed, for, standing where he asked me, a glare struck on the picture from the windows, and I could not see it. However, the request was reasonably made, and from a countryman; so I complied, and turning away, stood by his easel. I knew it was not worth while; yet I referred in some way to the work underneath the one he was copying. He did not laugh, but he smiled as we do in England. "*Very* odd, is it not?" said he.

The other students near us were all continental; and seeing an Englishman select an Englishman to speak with, conceived, I suppose, that he could understand no language but his own. They had evidently been noticing the interest which the little picture appeared to excite in me.

One of them, an Italian, said something to another who stood next to him. He spoke with a Genoese accent, and I lost the sense in the villainous dialect. "Che so?" relied the other, lifting his eyebrows toward the figure; "roba mistica: 'st' Inglesi son matti sul misticismo: somiglia alle nebbie di là. Li fa pensare alla patria, 'e intenerisce il core lo di ch' han detto ai dolci amici adio.' "

"La notte, vuoi dire," said a third.

There was a general laugh. My compatriot was evidently a novice in the language, and did not take in what was said. I remained silent, being amused.

"Et toi donc?" said he who had quoted Dante, turning to a student, whose birthplace was unmistakable, even had he been addressed in any other language: "que dis-tu de ce genre-là?"

"Moi?" returned the Frenchman, standing back from his easel, and looking at me and at the figure, quite politely, though with an evident reservation: "Je dis, mon cher, que c'est une spécialité dont je me fiche pas mal. Je tiens que quand on ne comprend pas une chose, c'est qu'elle ne signifie rien."

My reader thinks possibly that the French student was right.

The Two Partings

By William Morris

On Tuesday, the 13th, Helen, the beloved wife of Major Con-
way, aged 26.

Such was the first notice among the deaths in the *Times*, which
I was reading in a German hotel. Deeply did I ponder on that
word beloved, wondering whether it was a mere phrase of fashion, signifying nothing, or whether she, whose heart, when she
married, was mine, had yet been a faithful and loving wife, win-
ning thereby her husband's love in return. The 13th. Well did I
remember that day; for, on that day, four years ago, she and I
parted, to meet only once again. It was an old story. We had
loved each other deeply, it may be not wisely, but too well. She
was my first, as she has been hitherto my only, love. And so, for
many months we were very happy, and, living near each other,
were nearly always together. But, at last, in the early autumn, I
was obliged to leave her for a few weeks; and, in my absence, a
female friend told her—I could never learn exactly what; but the
point of it was, that I no longer loved her; and Helen's love for
me made her very jealous of my affection, unable to endure even
a suspicion of faithlessness in me, and so the whispering tongue
of the false friend, poisoned the truth—the truth of Helen and

me; for truly, indeed, did we love each other. She wrote to me a very strange letter, a curious mixture of warmth and coldness; with sentences that began most tenderly and ended with reproaches; concluding with a demand that I should see her as soon as I could. I hastened home immediately, without waiting even to reply to her letter, and called upon her at once. I had to walk nearly two miles. It was a dark, windy night, with occasional gleams of moonshine, in the middle of autumn. The wind raced madly over the level country, and tossed the bare arms of the trees about in a sort of rough wild play. The moon every now and then opened glaring rifts in the thick clouds, throwing black shadows on the ground, which moved restlessly as the trees rocked in the gusts. A rude night it was; yet to one who did not fear wind and cold, a pleasant night withal, rousing his strength and manliness by its rough visitation, and the sympathy between the spirit of man and the elements. Thus, when I saw a light in the house where Helen lived—in the very room where I thought she might be; strengthened and excited by my conflict with the fierce wind, I walked proudly and confidently, confident in the manhood which I knew to be in me; and which is so nearly allied with truthfulness. As I stood at the door, I heard her singing a very favourite song of ours, called "Faith." She was singing the last verse, and I waited till she had finished before I knocked.

> "No; 'tis not hand fast lock'd in hand,
>   Nor gaze of melting eyes,
> Nor lips that meet with lingering kiss,
>   Nor trembling, soft replies;
> 'Tis Faith that is the soul of love,
>   Firm, fearless, shaken never;
> Two hearts once join'd in one by faith,
>   Nor life nor death shall sever."

I took it as a good omen, and entered with a wonderfully light heart. She received me with her old warmth and tenderness, and we talked for a while without alluding to the subject which had brought me to her. At last, with an uneasy smile, far too significant, but which I could not modify, I introduced it.

"Who or what could have put into her head the strange notion that I no longer loved her?"

"She had been told so, and reasons had been given; but she did not feel justified in disclosing the name of her informant."

Then, conscious of my innocence, I disdained to defend myself, but commenced a bitter tirade against the mischievous tongue of the unknown false friend, which made her reply, angrily, "I will not have a friend abused to my face; it is for you to prove the assertions false, not rail against them."

This made me angry in my turn, and our explanation soon became mutual accusations and reproaches, which in her were cold and stinging, and in me were vehement and passionate, till at length she took from a book which I had given her, my last letter, and saying in a deliberate, though trembling, voice, "I will no longer submit to this; here, sir, is the letter I last received from you; the others I will send you in the morning," placed it on the table before me. I took it up,—the letter in which I had so lately called her my sweetest, and noblest, and best beloved,— and furiously tore it to pieces, which I dashed about the room. With that assumption of dignity and self-respect so common in women, she said in a tone that was now quite cold and firm, "Sir, I should have thought you would have had more self-command, if not more respect for me. Leave me at once, and let me never see you again."

Then, wrathful and impassioned, I spoke with loud vehemence in which my whole heart was poured out.

"Helen, Helen, do not drive me mad by this wicked, heartless woman's pride. I will leave you; I will never see you again. I will thank God, night and day, that he has opened my eyes to your faithlessness before it was too late. I will tear out all remembrance of you. Fool, fool that I am—I am almost mad; my heart overflows with bitterness, through you, whom once I loved so truly and tenderly."

Oh could I have looked at her with eyes that could judge impartially; for I still remember—I shall never forget— how I vaguely seemed to see in her a sort of hesitation, an involuntary hurried movement towards me; but I hastily turned away, and left her—I thought for ever; but it proved only for years, but years that were long and weary enough. And some time in the course of those years some one told me how, while I was standing near the door of the house, till now the gate of heaven to me, but now for ever closed upon me, though I could not but linger still near it, she threw herself on the sofa, weeping and sobbing violently, then gathered up the fragments of my letter, and kissed them passionately. Oh, in this world of error and wrong, we hear what should have been kept silent; and what should have been made known, we hear not, or hear too late. Had they told me this then, when only it could have availed, my first love and I had never parted thus, to meet for a little time years after, and then part for ever.

Out again, in the wild night, with the boisterous wind playing roughly around me as before; but it seemed no longer play to me now, but was stern, though apparently aimless, earnest,—like my own thoughts, which were all in a whirl, with only one thing stedfast, the resolution not to be overcome, even by lost love. So I walked on wildly in the wild night, almost running, mad with excitement, with the world before me; for it was plain that I could no longer live where I had lived before, so near Helen. I soon made up my mind to leave England altogether, and then very soon fixed on Germany as my future country; partly because I expected to find the German character, of all the continental nations, most akin to the English, and partly because I wished to increase a knowledge, already extensive, of German literature.

While I was making my preparations, and while I was travelling, and even for some time after I had settled in my new country, the excitement and the novelty distracted my thoughts; and, though they could not make me happy, left me not at leisure to be miserable. But when I was fairly settled, and the new scenes and faces began to grow familiar to me, as they very soon did, then I had leisure to turn my thoughts inwards, and soon I did little else than brood alone over my woe.

For six long months, I was as one stunned, caring for nothing, heeding nothing; then despair gradually settled into deep melancholy, and I felt that my only remedy lay in constant action, to keep off the thoughts that I durst not face. So I worked on steadily for three years, writing much, and reading more, and mixing much with men, not only with my equals in rank, but also entering the abodes of the poor and needy, and aiding and comforting them as well as I could. And before long I began to find the reward of my exertions in a peace of mind which continually increased, though with occasional ebbs; and sometimes I even gained glimpses of the solution of that which was the great question of my life, why Helen had been of so little faith towards me. Verily, it was a fearful problem, and one which I could never wholly solve; usually I fled from it, and blindly trusted and hoped, though often it was a sore grief and temptation that I could not see the end and know the good.

And not a day passed on which I did not think of her, some days for hours; belying that futile boast of my hot youth, proud of its strength of will, that I would never think of her again.

LOST LOVE

Fix'd in my breast the arrow stood,
 The shaft of thy untruth:
I said, with all the bitter fire,
 The frenzied pride of youth:

"I loved thee as my life, but now
 My love at once is o'er;
The heart thy sudden falsehood wrung,
 Thou shalt wring never more.

Even now, I fling thee all away,
 All memory, all regret,
The past a dream, and we who loved
 Like those who never met."

O vain, vain boast of madden'd youth!
 The years still roll away,
And bring new pains and hopes and joys,
 But never yet the day,

That fills not all my soul with thee,
With longing, love and woe;
Lost, lost, but loved, as in the years
So strange, so long ago.

Would it have been better had I forgotten her? Or did those thoughts, so varied, sad, sometimes bitter, but generally hopeful, at least trustful, work some great work within me, and make me fitter for—? Do souls parted here, souls that have really loved each other, do they ever renew and accomplish their love in the ages of the great eternity? At least hope on, hope and trust, though to the end of life. But my loss, borne with whatsoever fortitude, leavened my whole life, and in the dimness of my sorrow all things wore a sorrowful look; and I saw the pain and the grief far more readily than the pleasure and the joy; and I heard how, day by day, yea, night by night, rose up from all the earth the cry of woe to the thrones of God— woe diverse as the fortunes of men; famished moans from those who starved in deserts and villages, far from help; yea, and in great cities, too, in the very midst of overflowing wealth; groans of pain from the sick and the maimed and the dying; the low complaining of discontent, not only from the cottage and the alley, but from mansions and palaces also: the one continual undertone of sadness from the hearts whose light, like mine, had been darkened by one great disappointment, one great sorrow, struggled against, borne stoutly and sternly through the long years, but never healed: for ever, day after day, the myriad-toned cry went up. And yet the glad bosom of the earth bore corn-fields and rice-fields, the oak and the alder, the rose and the lily; and the grand solemn cathedrals still stood, on the green sward and in the paved square, stately and strong, for ages; and the proud palaces, reared gay or sombre fronts, high over the misery; and music, awful and holy from mighty organs in dim churches, weird and wondrous, from horn and violin in painted halls, festive and merry in bright saloons—sometimes sad too, but still sweet and beautiful, ever sounded on; and the voices of parents and children, brothers and sisters, friends and lovers talked, low and tenderly, with words of trust and affection; and the war-shouts of giant nations thundered to the booming and crashing of cannon and shell. And still, amid all the beauty and grandeur, amid the sweet and beautiful music, and the tender talking of love, and the roar of battle, went up for ever that voice of multitudinous woe, wailing and mourning, and deep lamentation. Neither would the riddle of the painful earth give one sign, even a hint of solution,—a voiceless, motionless, passionless sphinx—sitting, for ever, in the desert of life—perplexing, mocking, torturing me; to me, as to thousands, both now and of old, the good and the evil, the beautiful and the ugly, the grand and the mean—existing, working side by side, not in harmony, but in a sort of discordant union, which seemed as if it could never be broken, yet never be made into order. And from the depths of my soul came ever the still, small cry, how long? how long?

At length, about three years after our separation, I was obliged to return to England; and, one evening, was at a party, at the house of Captain Dalton. Early in the evening, the hostess came up to me, and, smiling somewhat significantly, said, "Mr. Gordon, I want to introduce you to an old friend; come with me."

I expected to see an old school-fellow; but it was a lady, whom I almost immediately recognized as Helen. I started back, feeling all the blood go from my cheeks, and gasping for breath. She scarcely suppressed a cry of surprise; and, when I looked at her again, was as pale as death. Mrs. Dalton, of course, perceived our emotion, but she left us to ourselves. Helen soon recovered, and had bowed with tolerable self-possession; for, I scarcely know why, we did not shake hands. For a few moments we remained silent, not knowing what to say. She was the first to speak.

"Have you been in England long?"

"About a fortnight;" and then came another pause.

"I am glad to see you," she said presently, with a smile so constrained and sad, that it filled me at once with pity and dread. But it broke the spell that was upon me, and I said, earnestly, "Helen, do not let us lose this happy opportunity. Come with me into that room, and let us speak out our hearts to each other."

She accompanied me into the room which I pointed out, and which was at the present quite unoccupied. I locked the door, and began at once with a vehemence that made my voice quaver.

"O Helen, I cannot tell you how I have longed for this time. I knew it would come, though it has been so long coming; and, now, I must speak out and tell you all. Through all the long years that we have been parted, I have striven to forget you. You remember, perhaps, what I said on that last miserable night, that I would never think of you again. Oh! how little I knew my own heart then! Not a day has passed in which I have not thought much about you; and almost always tenderly. And now, meeting you again so suddenly, I will not say that my old love has returned, but I feel that the love which has never ceased can no longer be repressed."

I stretched forth my hand, as if to take her own, but she held it still by her side; and I now saw that she was trembling violently.

"O Arthur, Arthur," at length she sobbed, "why did you return? Or, why did we not meet a year ago? Now it is too late. Oh! it is fearful, fearful. We must never meet again. In a month I am to be married."

My heart seemed to stop its beating at those words; and, for several moments, I stood quite quiet, in calm despair. Then I heard her say, again, "Yes, go at once; it will be best for both. That it should have come to this! This is worse even than I thought it would be. Say good bye at once, and leave me for ever."

Tears choked her voice, but I durst not console her. I took her hand (she gave it me at last), the hand I once knew so well; hot tears—I could not check them—fell upon it, as I pressed it, oh how passionately and hopelessly! then I forced myself to say, "Good bye, good bye," gazing the while into her deep blue eyes, the eyes that I was never more to look into; and, in another minute was out of the house.

Back again to my adopted country, with my grief renewed and intensified—grief that threatened to become despair; only, the self-command that I had gained in the fearful struggle of the previous three years saved me, and before long brought me back my old tranquillity,—peace of mind, however sad, and even stern. But she;—how did she bear it?

Married to another, when her heart was mine. But why think

of that? I could not help her, save by my prayers, which I offered up for her night and day; but, otherwise, I could not aid her. For, however much we may bear each other's burdens; yet, in this world of isolation every heart must know its own sorrow. Moreover, cruel Absence and Time put ever a greater distance between us; and though they could never lessen my love, yet they took, ever more and more, her presence from me; so that I forgot the face that was once the most beautiful thing in the world to me, and the voice that sounded sweetest in my ear. And now, for long months, until this morning, it had seemed all a dream. The past existed for me only historically, the few incidents that I could still recollect, no longer bringing back the old feelings with them. Alas, alas! it is the greatest triumph of Time, this destruction of old feelings, even when the events are left in; when the pressure of the hand is still remembered, but the thrill that it shot through the pulses quickens the blood no more. It is then that the past seems most utterly gone from us; gone, wholly, and for ever. And, it is only a month since I wrote this song, when Helen seemed to me almost like some maiden in the Tales of the Thousand and One Nights:

LOVE LONG AGO

Did I dream it in my sleep?
    Did they tell me when a boy?
Or have I read it in some tale
    Of forgotten love and joy?

For it seems that I was loved,
    That I loved, I know not when;
But the time was long ago,
    And will never come again.

I have mourn'd o'er tales of love,
    I have wept in my dreams;
I was sure some dream or tale,
    So far and strange it seems.

> Far and strange, and faint;
>   But it haunts me night and day
> With thoughts that look like memories
>   Of the years that have passed away.

And I know, too, that soon this vividness of memory will fade also; and her face and voice again become a shadow and an echo to me; but I know, also, that henceforth she will be ever present to me; not to eye and ear, but spirit to spirit; present to me through all my life. And, when death shall take me away from earth, God grant I may find that I have died into Life and Love; for the consummation has at length come; and Helen is once more mine, and I am hers.

The Druid
and the Maiden

By Edward Burne-Jones

"It is a wild corner of earth, this Brittany. It lies like a dead branch on a green elm, or a burial-ground in the middle of a huge city, the great fossil of the past in the very lap of the civilized world. And how is it that Brittany seems scarcely to have altered since the days of Caesar? how is it that it has defied canals and railroads, that the vulgar slang of the nineteenth century—that paragon of progress!—has not polluted its hills and vales, that it is useless, manufactureless, unheeded in your exhibitions and annual reports, uncared for by the speculator, and spurned by the hack traveller? Is it not that the Present with all its achievements, its men turned to machines, and its machine-turned men—with all its powers of motion and creation, this newspaper present that sings its own praises till hoarse in the throat—blushes before the long-forgotten, unknown Past, which in one thing at least has outdone it? Is it not ashamed to bring its patent-leather boots over the ground, where a wondrous race once trod,—a race which possessed a mighty secret we cannot solve, unless forsooth it was a race of giants, of

79

Anakim—and has left its mighty works to stand, not for ages only, but as long as Earth shall last? Thank Heaven, there is at least one spot of Earth left, and that, too, no distant desert, but within a day's journey, where this vile, fresh-paint odour of the new age cannot reach us!"

Thus I mused, as with knapsack on my back, and a railing misanthropy in my heart, I wandered over the wild hills of Brittany. I had just left Carnac—wonderful Carnac!—that petrified army—those rows of a thousand stones, brought no one knows whence, no one knows how, no one now knows why, and set upright in long, straight ranks, by a people who flourished some two thousand years gone, of whose existence and glory nought now remains but a few wild legends and these huge unmeaning stones.

I had caught my first view of the Atlantic, that eternity of waves, the boundary of the ancient, the highway of the modern, world,—and stretching far away into it I had seen the long, bleak spit of Quiberon, where a little faithful band of Royalists had once landed, full of hope, full of courage, full of confidence in English protection, and little dreaming of English mismanagement, to be cut to pieces by a band of ruthless revolutionists. I passed on to Locmariaquer.

From the hill above the little desolate village, I looked down on the bright inland sea of Morbihan, rushing fiercely in from the Atlantic through a gate of rocks, and studded with a hundred islands. Nay, the fishermen declare that there are as many rocky isles within it as the days of the year. It was a bright sunset. The cloudlets circled golden around the sinking day-god, like angels round a dying man, and the last red beams purpled the cliffs of the foremost islands, with the breakers of the Atlantic dashing at their feet.

In a few minutes I rushed down the hill into the village of fishermen's huts, and ere long had hired a sailingboat to take me over to Gavr Inis, or the beautiful island.

Two honest Breton sailors were all the crew of the little bark.

"We must make the best of our time," said one of them to me; "for, fair as it is now, there will be a breeze up before the sun is down. We can run over in half an hour, for the wind is with us, but when you have seen the cave, we shall have barely time to weather back again."

I leapt into the boat, the broad sail was hoisted, and away we went, heaving and dashing through the blue waves. The men sat down and pulled out their pipes. I did the same, and offered them some English tobacco, which was much finer than their own, and thus paved the way to a lively conversation.

"It's a good country, is England, sir," said one of them in a large tarpaulin hat. "I spent a long time at Southampton, in the last war. I was on board a French corvette that was cruising in the Channel, and we all got taken prisoners. But I never spent a better time in my life. They treated me wondrous well, and I like your beer a deal better than our cider here."

He was a weather-beaten man of about sixty. The other, who was younger, listened to him with respect.

"Tell the gentleman," said he, "how it was you made friends over there."

"Ay, ay, that was a curious business. I was only a boy then, and we were being marched up to Southampton, and there were a couple of others from these parts with me. We were laughing and talking a good deal together in Gallic, and making a pretty good noise, when up comes the sergeant of the escort and calls out something to the soldiers who were with us, meaning to keep us quiet. 'Agh,' cried I in Breton, 'it's a shame that we should not be allowed the freedom of tongue, when every other kind of freedom is taken from us.' The sergeant turned round, and looked quite astonished: 'Arragh,' cries he, in my own language, 'you're not from Ireland, my lads, are ye?' 'That we're not, indeed, God be praised,' answered I; 'but it seems you're from Brittany, for you speak the same as we do.' And sure enough he turned in and had a long chat with us, and that's the first time I found out that the Irish people talked Gallic."

"But surely," said I, "there is a great difference between Breton and Irish."

"Not so much tho', sir. They have many words that we could not understand, and some of our words they pronounce differently, but we could understand each other well enough; and the sergeant, who was the only Irishman in the company, and was

glad to talk a bit in his own tongue, was our friend ever afterwards, and many a good turn he served us."

"And what kind of a cave is this on Gavr Inis?" I asked.

"Well, sir, it's a wonderful place. It was cut, so they say, many a
hundred year ago by our forefathers, who, I've heard tell, were
once kings of France, and England too,—right into the living
rock. You go in by a little hole, that a fox might make, and climb
down into a long passage quite in the middle of the hill, where
you could not see your hand before you without a light."

"Then you have brought lights with you, I suppose?"

"Oh yes, sir, a candle a-piece. You'll see a hole cut out in the
stone of one of the sides, where they say they used to tie a man's
hands behind his back, and sacrifice him to some of their gods,
sir; for it seems they were not Christians at that time."

There was a short silence. I was thinking whether any reliance
could be placed on this local legend, whether the nature-worship
of the Druid had ever descended to human sacrifice, as their
enemies indeed have averred, but which we have so little reliable
authority for believing.

My train of thought was suddenly interrupted by a loud cry in
Breton, and the next moment the sail swung round, the beam
struck me on the back of the head and threw me into the bottom
of the boat. When I had scrambled up again, I saw the two men
anxiously labouring to manage the sail. We were in a whirlwind;
the waves were rising higher and higher, and a huge cloud,
which five minutes before had been scarcely noticed in the distance, was driving rapidly towards us, and covering the whole
heavens with its black wings.

"We shall have a bit of a squall," cried one of the men to me.
"But it will not last. Will you take the rudder, sir, a moment or
two, while we manage to tack about?"

"Don't you think we could run back again to Locmariaquer?" I
replied, going to the stern. "We can give up the attempt to reach
the island to-night, and try again to-morrow morning."

"It's impossible, sir," answered the sailor. "We should only be
running into the thick of the storm, and we can reach the island
in five minutes, if we can only manage the wind. You see it there,
sir? well, steer right at that white point, and—"

Whatever he might have said, was lost in the hurricane that came down upon us. The rain rushed pelting down; the whole air was black around us; in another minute the sail was down, and the two men were working lustily at the oars against wave and wind.

I could just see the white speck through the darkness, and I steered straight ahead towards it. We were making some way, and the white rock, for such it seemed to be, was nearer and nearer. But the waves broke in upon the boat, heavy tub though it was, and completed the wetting that the rain had already given me.

"Steer out, steer out, sir, a bit, not too much. Out, out, sir, quick. There are hidden rocks here: ah!— "

At this instant a huge wave broke right upon us. For a moment I was blinded by the water, and when I recovered my sight I saw that we were close in upon a shore, girt with a bed of low rocks, just peeping above the retiring waves. The next moment there was a crack, and the handle of the rudder was torn from my hand, while the boat nearly capsized. I got on my knees with the speed of lightning to try and recover my hold of the rudder, when to my utter discomfiture I saw it a yard or two behind us dashed about in the foam of a huge breaker.

"The rudder is gone," I cried, turning round, and saw the younger of the men leap from the boat upon the rocks with the painter in his hand, while the other was endeavouring to keep the boat clear with an oar.

The young man leapt fearlessly from rock to rock in the surge. He must have known the spot well, for it was quite dark, and by dragging the boat along, he at last brought the boat's head on to the bank. Two or three rapidly succeeding waves drove us with violent shocks up the stones. The old man leapt out into the shallow surge; I followed his example, and in a few minutes our united efforts had dragged the skiff high and dry up the shingle.

"Well, now," said I, when the boat was secured, "we must look out for a place of shelter, for this rain will last several hours yet, in spite of the wind. Which is the way up to the cave?"

The old man, to whom I put this question, looked confused.

"Monsieur does not wish to see the cave to-night?"

"Why not? I intend to sleep there for an hour or two, so as to be out of the wet."

The two men looked at one another oddly.

"Monsieur will not sleep much, I am thinking," said the younger one.

"Not sleep? what do you mean? I am sure I am tired enough."

The old man scratched his head and looked perplexed.

"There was never anybody slept in that cave yet," he resumed.

"Ah! I see, you have some stories about it, eh?"

The old fellow looked down obliquely.

"Well," I continued, "we shall be three together. We can't come to much harm. Come, a stout old fellow like you!"

The old man only looked foolish.

"No, sir," said the younger one, "I don't mind showing you the way up there, but I and my partner here will sleep outside, if you please. We shall get shelter enough under the shrubs about there."

"Move on, then," I said, internally grumbling at their obstinate superstitions, and rather gloating over the prospect of doing what they said nobody had ever done before, and so proving to them that they were wrong.

We had to climb a long way in the dark, up a steep, winding path, where my hands came into as frequent use as my feet. We were nearly half an hour getting up, and I was not a little torn and bruised, when we reached a kind of landing-place some yards below the top of the rocky hill.

Short, thick shrubs surrounded this place on every side. The sailors advanced slowly together towards a place where the gorse and the shrubs were thickest, and beckoned to me to follow them.

"Here, sir," said the old man, "put these in your pocket: you may want them." So saying, he gave me a short piece of a tallow candle, and a small iron box full of lucifers.

I crept in on hands and knees through the opening which they made by holding the shrubs back, and soon found I was able to stand upright on a hard pavement of stone.

I struck one of my lucifers and lit the candle. The light was dim and illumined a space of about a yard round me, not more.

Beyond this, the darkness seemed even thicker than before. I was in a kind of passage, about six feet high and seven broad. The walls consisted of large flat stones, and as I passed the candle along them, I saw to my astonishment a series of the most elegant serpentine designs, graven in single lines over the whole surface. On each stone the pattern was different, but still in each there was a certain resemblance to the twisted form of the snake, which I remembered was an animal of deep symbolical import among the old Druids.

I sang out "*Bon soir*," before I passed on, imagining that the sailors would hear me. But my voice range like a bell from wall to wall with a hollow ding-dong noise, and I waited in vain for an answer.

I confess that this feeling of loneliness, and the terror of the two Bretons, had an effect on me as I groped along, and this increased when, after some yards of the passage, I found myself within a loftier hall. It was not large, it is true. There was room perhaps for some dozen people to stand, but the strange devices on the walls seemed to call up the Past to people it with shades.

I groped round it. The cave ended here, and the only thing that broke the monotony of the graven stones above, below, and around me, was a curious double niche cut out on one side. It was so managed as to leave a strong stone bar in the middle.

Here then was the place to which the sailor had referred. Here it was, to this stone bar, that the human victim was tied, and between those stones in the floor his blood must have flowed away.

I set my candle in this niche, took off my cloak, laid it upon the ground, and prepared to make myself as cozy as possible, by divesting my shivering limbs of their dripping nether garments. I kept the rest of my clothes on to guard again the cold, and lying down, covered my legs with my cloak.

The candle was already burning low, for there was not much of it, and the darkness grew closer and closer about me, as I thought dreamily on all the old tales I had ever heard of the Druids and the Celts in general. I was rather excited by the events of the evening, and it was evident that I could not sleep soundly.

From time to time I dozed a little, while the light still burned, and was annoyed with those funny dreams one has now and then, of being at a large party in my actual costume, and not discovering till I had waltzed once or twice, that my lower limbs were bereft of the garments which society requires to be worn. I would wake up at the moment of a desperate attempt to put on my trowsers, which always proved futile.

At length the last flicker of the candle blazed up, and the next moment I was left to doze in utter darkness. Whether I was awake or not I knew not, but my ears, at least, were not shut, and the sound of a wild distant song came up the passage. It seemed to be the mingled voices of men and women. It grew nearer and nearer, and at last resounded in the passage itself. I remembered turning on my side, and then I felt cold drops of sweat rise at the roots of my hair, my flesh crept, my arm clung powerless to my side, and my legs bent up under me.

Two tapers were dimly glittering at the bottom of the passage, and behind them two shadowy figures, clothed in long white robes, slowly and solemnly moved towards me.

My heart stopped beating; my breath hovered in my throat. The figures moved on, and behind them I could see some dozen others, all in long white robes.

They came and came, nearer and nearer, and at last filled the chamber where I lay. Then the low wild music ceased, and one of the two foremost raised his lank arms and fell flat on his face before me. My eyes closed, and again all was dark.

When I opened them again the forms were gone.

For some minutes I scarcely dared to move. I am one of those strong-minded people who will never believe in "humbugs" of this kind. I had been accustomed to run down everything in which imagination seemed to play any prominent part. But this was the first trial my principles had received, and I must confess it converted me for the moment even in spite of myself. I knew not what to believe, but I perfectly knew what I felt. And yet, surely, I thought, it must be a dream, or an hallucination—of course it must. So I rubbed my eyes to see whether I was awake or not, and certainly believed that I was wide awake.

At last I summoned courage to turn my eyes round in their

sockets, (for hitherto they had remained paralyzed with an undefined fear,) and as I did so I started to see almost close to my side something long and white upon the floor. This time I was less frightened, for I had got accustomed to unwonted sights.

But whatever the prostrate mass might be, it was not content to remain prostrate. It rose slowly and stood at last before me, by my side, almost over me. It was the form of a man in his thirtieth year, tall, majestic, handsome. A loose dress of white linen fell from his neck to his feet, and was girt at the waist with a band of twisted tender oak sprigs. The robe was sleeveless, and his bare arms were muscular, though white. His face was handsome, with high intellectual, almost noble, features; but there was an expression about his eyes of cunning foiled and shamed, ambition disappointed, and selfish intrigue worked up to the crisis of crime.

The reader will be wondering—though, for my part, I had no wonder to spare on such a trifle *then*—how in the thick darkness of the cave I could manage to see all these details. This question would pose me. Gentle reader, have you ever seen a ghost? Have you ever passed a night with the shade of a reanimated Druid priest? No? well then, I cannot help it. I must wait till your turn comes, when you will perfectly appreciate the kind of invisible halo that surrounds an incorporeal being, and fully understand what I cannot, for the life of me, explain.

I have described the phantom's expression, that is, the expression which his character had imprinted on his features; but I have not added, that at this moment he wore one of intense melancholy besides.

He was turned towards me, and was looking at me. This did not now disquiet me; but still my tongue refused to move and demand, as I longed to do, who it was that I spoke to. He saved me the trouble, however, by quietly sitting down beside me, which sent a new thrill of agitation through my body.

"Does he sleep?" he muttered low, though in what language I cannot say. I only know that I understood him very well, so that it must have been either French or English.

"And who," he continued, "is brave enough to break upon my solitude, to seek the Druid in his den, and bring the vulgar Pres-

ent to the shadows of the Past? Is not the temple which my own
father built, the shrine I hallowed with HIS blood"—here he
buried his face in his hands, and was silent a moment—"is not
this of right our own? Why then does the stranger, rather than
our own descendants, who speak our tongue, seek our haunts to
lay his head in? Stranger!"

I muttered a trembling "Yes."

"So you are come to see the famous Gavr Inis, the beautiful
island? Well, you do well to come by night, for its glory is departed."

"Ichabod, Ichabod," I murmured instinctively.

"But," he continued, not heeding my little remark, "it once
merited its name. It once *was* the beautiful island indeed, the
loveliest of three hundred and sixty-five that spring within this
inland sea. Here the oak forest was thicker, here the mistletoe
more luxurious—"

"So that you might have had Christmas twice a year," I
thought, with a little chuckle, but said nothing.

"—The wood-flowers bore a fresher bloom, the shepherd warriors were stouter and more terrible, and the shepherd maidens
fairer to look upon than in all the land of the Celts. But now,
alas! how changed!—"

By this time I had become quite myself again. But it was with a
frightful effort that I brought my voice to my lips.

"May I ask"—again I paused—"are you—a—a Druid?"

"I was a Druid. I am now what you see me."

"And that is?—"

"A Spirit of the Past."

There was such a solemnity in the voice with which he uttered
these words that a strong desire to laugh, which my "common
sense" roused in me, was nipped in the bud.

I looked at the strange being with respect and awe.

"What brings you here to-night?" I asked, timidly.

"A crime committed on this day nineteen centuries ago. For
twenty centuries I was condemned to revisit the spot where I had
shed innocent blood, once a year, and to pass my night in the
torture of memory. Every circumstance of my life on earth is

now recalled; its neglected opportunities, its happiness too soon blighted, its—its—crimes—"

I raised myself on my elbow. I felt an interest in, almost a sympathy for, the man of so strange a fate.

"It might perhaps soften this pain of recollection, to tell your tale to an interested listener."

His eyes turned obliquely towards me, with a slight look of suspicion. Then he smiled a melancholy smile.

"There was a time," he said, "when I should have suspected some latent motive in your suggestion. Now, how can you, how can any mortal harm me? What are my confidences now—known as they are in heaven? It would relieve my sorrow. I will tell you my tale.

"My father was the Arch-Druid of the province. Carnac, even then, had passed into a mystery. The Dolar Marchant, as you now call it, was the great resort of the members of the college, because the great menhir—alas! alas! thrown down and shivered now into three huge pieces—was close to it. My father lived at yonder village, Cœr-Bhelen, we called it, and now 'tis named Locmariaquer. Yes, Bhelen, the great, the noble, had given place to a woman!

"At my birth, a wandering bard came from the south. He struck his lyre of the triple chord and sang:

'Woe to the child when the Eagle's
      wings
    Shall darken the skies of the north;
Woe to the child when Venetan kings
    To battle shall march forth.
An eaglet's blood shall stain his hand,
    A woman lead the host,
A maiden's death-shriek fill the land,
    And the Druid's rule be lost.'

"My father loved me none the less for the evil omen. I was his only child, and at an early age he taught me all the awful legends of the truth. I was a silent wondering boy, and I grasped eagerly after knowledge. The science of the stars, the science of the world, the science of the great invisible soul of nature,—such were my early studies.

"He sent me, at fifteen, to Alesia. At the Sacred College I was marked as the student who knew most, and learned most; and when I left it, proud in my honours, I stood before the whole college of Druids, and swore by Esus, by Bhelen and by Thiutath—what oath could have been greater?—that I would never forsake its cause, and that day and night I would strive to preserve the great religion.

"I returned home with the oak-wreath on my brows—a priest. I took ship at Wenedh (Venetum), to cross to Cœr-Bhelen. A storm arose, and we put in at this very island. From a child I knew it well. I had often sought it in my father's boat with its red sails of hide.

"The next day I learnt that the gathering of the Vervain was to take place on the island. I felt a natural pride to show the inhabitants my newly-won oak-wreath, and I stayed for it. For this ceremony a company of virgins is chosen, and the youngest maiden culls the little herb.

"Beneath the spreading oaks they came. A lovelier band was never gathered on green sward, and yet she who led them was lovelier than all the rest. She was a girl of fifteen summers, and still looked a child in form and bearing. She came on, timid as a young fawn, and blushing at every step. It was a lovely sight, such as I may never see again—alas! Each maiden wore a robe of flowing white linen, girt below the breast, and sweeping, not clinging, around her form. In their long locks were woven bands of spring flowers, and their hair, each one's silkier than the other's, each one's of another hue, flowed down their young shoulders, and courted the sunbeams with their gloss. Their white arms were bare, and a gold bracelet, pliable, and simple, clasped the tender flesh above the elbow.

"But she—ah! Dona!—she, lovelier in her childish form, lovelier in her modest face, lovelier in her timid gait—with the young knowledge struggling with the child's innocence in her tender bosom—than all the rest, came on through the thick wood, with the sunbeams gilding one leaf and forsaking another, brightening one lock of hair, and deepening the shade of the next, and chequering the briary ground beneath her bare feet, small and tender as young rosebuds—and looked from right to left to find the sacred herb. A young Druid, whom I knew well, bore the basket before the troop, and on either side the islanders accompanied them.

"Suddenly, she started from the path, and darting with the fire of heaven in her soul among the briars and brambles which tore her white feet, she burst out with the first note of the holy hymn. All the voices took it up. An old bard stepped from the crowd and struck his lyre to the air.

"Then, as they sang, she stooped. With her left hand she put back the long brown locks that fell across her shoulders, and curving the little finger of the right hand, she culled the sacred herb with it alone. No other finger touched it, as she rose and dropped it into the basket of the young Druid.

"The ceremony was over, and we returned to the village. As we went, I asked the Druid, my friend, who the maiden was.

" 'You,' he answered, you, newly come, pride-laden from Alesia, know all that the Roman is doing in the South. I need not tell you that Caesar is driving all before him, northwards. Well, this maid, who is indeed a gem of beauty, has fled from the neighbourhood of Bibracte with her aged mother. She tells how her life—her honour even—was saved by a Roman knight, and how she staid not till they reached these hills, whither the southron will find it hard to penetrate.'

"Need I tell you that I fell enamoured of this damsel? Need I say how often I spread the red hide-sail to the northern breeze, and sought Gavr Inis and the smile of the lovely Dona?

"But I found her cold. My honours seemed little in her sight—myself nothing. Still I hoped. She was young, and I had nought but a student's glory to recommend me. I was fired with the ambition of love. I resolved to win a name in the province, for I saw that she loved the great and noble.

"A year passed, and the Roman Eagle again darkened the land with his huge wings. Julius Caesar was a name which all had heard, and heard with horror. I became popular by my working. I laboured hard among the people. I kept up the falling faith. I incited them to prepare for war. I collected the priests and the chieftains, and we trained the people to the bow and the axe. Everywhere I exclaimed proudly, 'the Celt shall never be a slave.'

"But the sky was dark. Another year and Vercingetorix was the name which resounded louder than that of Caesar in our hills. The news came that Alesia was besieged. All trusted to the noble band of Vercingetorix. But how was it that a melancholy silence fell on Dona when she heard the tidings? What was she meditating in that maiden breast? These two years had altered her. She was no longer the timid girl, she was rising to ambitious womanhood; she was reserved and pensive.

"At last my ambition called me to Wenedh, and I was parted for many a month from Dona.

"One day a man rode headlong into Wenedh, covered from heel to head with dirt and dust. His horse dropped dead beneath him.

"The townsmen crowded round him, and then, with sad voice, he declared that Alesia was fallen, and Vercingetorix was lost.

"The news flew like wildfire. My father came among the first from Locmariaquer. In every quarter we sent for every bowman that could still fix an arrow. Wenedh was crowded. The capital of our hill country, it was always the trysting place in times of danger. And now the whole country poured into it; some to see their friends depart for the war, some from curiosity, some to hear the news, and some even to offer their arms in their country's cause.

"A motley crowd assembled in the little market-place. The wild wood-cutters from the hills, with their axes across their swarthy arms; the peasant from the plains, with nought but a hide to cover him; the priest and the Druid in his long flowing garment of white linen; and the herdsman from the island, in his rough breeks of sheep-skin. Some from the neighbourhood still held a yoke of oxen by the horns, in such haste had they come; and others from hunting the wolf, had rushed hurriedly in with the heavy hang-jawed hounds still prancing on before them. All were asking, all stupidly waiting to see what would happen, all thinking that, because the capital was taken, the Roman must of course be on their threshold. Poor things, they knew not whether Alesia were one or ten days' journey from them.

"But the market-place was thronged the day after the news had come. The noise of oxen, horses, dogs and men was terrific. A large body of Druids had assembled, and my father had consulted with them what was to be done, and had agreed to harangue the people.

"We formed in procession and walked slowly, and with the sound of the mournful lyre, to the market-place. The crowd opened and knelt as we passed, and my father passed his thin white hands to and fro to bless them.

"He was very old, and his white hair danced about his temples like flakes of snow. Mounting a large stone in the middle of the place, he called on the folk to pray with him to Bhelen.

"He rose to address them, when the prayer was done, but, whether from age, or the excitement, his voice faltered and clung to his jaws. The people murmured, and looked down, and I was just going to come forward and lend the old man my voice, when I saw the farthermost of the crowd turning round, and looking up the road. The next moment I heard the hard rattle of hoof and stone. All the crowd turned to the quarter whence the noise came. A moment more, and the women were shrieking, and pulling back their children; the crowd opened and three horsemen dashed madly up to the stone where we stood.

"There was a moment's silence. Each man was straining his ears. Then the foremost of the three horsemen standing up in his stirrups, took his lance in his hand and brandished it furiously over his head.

" 'Men of Wenedh,' he cried in a voice of thunder, 'the Roman is coming. A Roman legion has crossed the Sechen. Their van is even now only five days hence. The chieftains have fallen back on the hills, and they call on you in the name of Thiutath, of Bhelen, of Esus to march out to their aid—ye and all the land. Men of Wenedh, arise!'

"A deathlike silence hung upon these words; they had taken the breath of all away. It lasted a minute, and then one wild shriek, one bitter wail from all the women, one mass of shouting, and loud defiant talking from the men filled the whole air.

" 'The Roman coming here? Caesar? the Eagle? the black Eagle with its talons and jaws streaming already with our blood? oh! terrible! terrible!'

"A panic had fallen on all. Alesia was gone, the country had lost its corner-stone. Still they had hoped to stand. They had thought that the Roman would have been sated with the pillage of the capital, and the autumn was coming on. Another month, and the careful Romans would have been gathering into winter-quarters. 'But, oh! oh! they are coming hither; death, slavery, pillage; our wives, our children slain or dishonoured before our eyes, our hearths polluted, our homes destroyed, ourselves in bondage!'

"Such was the thought of each, the thought that overpowered them, for they knew how terrible the Roman was, and shrank from the awful vision of Death.

"I saw that now was my moment. I rose upon the broad stone, flung my hands forward, and summoning all my voice, I cried, 'Celts, are ye ready to defend the land?'

"A murmur,—I had expected a loud reply of 'Yes,'—but only a murmur, low, grumbling, and wretched, followed my words. Then I know not what I said. I conjured them by all that was most holy, most dear, by their very name of Celt, to rise and strike for home, for life. But, oh! when fear possesses a whole crowd, there is no rousing them. I called them cowards. There was a low murmur, but nothing more. Just then my eyes fell on a distant corner, whither they had not wandered before.

"I saw a lovely face with blue eyes strained in anxious stare, the dark brown locks now hanging on the back, the slender neck stretching forward, the curved nostril of the high nose dilating with passion,—one hand resting on the stone on which she sat, the other seeming each moment to clutch at some visionary thing at her side, the little bosom heaving, throbbing, swelling quick and warm,—and this was Dona.

"Her eyes were on me, and seemed to call me. I gathered up my whole force and cried, 'Once more I call you, brothers—once more, and then your blood, your children's, wives' and mothers' blood be on your own heads,' and sank down, filled with the gaze of Dona. Oh! her eyes bright with ambition, glittering with her people's love, wild with suppressed indignation, called me, inspired me, pleaded to me—to *me*, whom she had almost scorned. I was drowning in my reverie, when I heard the deep vibration of the harp beside me. I turned, and Cervorix, the bard who had chanted the evil omen at my birth, was spreading his broad hand and branching fingers over the chords.

> 'Celt, is the war-axe whetted,
>> Celt, is the arrow bright,
> To pierce the Southern Eagle's heart?
>> Rise, Celt, march on and fight.
> Fight for thy land, thy home, thy wife;
>> Wield strong the glittering glaive;
> Shed the warm blood, fling down the life;
>> But scorn to be a slave!
> What! shall the Roman triumph,
>> And trample on the name
> Which echoed once from sea to sea,
>> The Gallic warrior's fame?
> Shall your sons curse the cowards
>> That dared not meet the foe?
> And bondsmen, rattling chains, mock out,
>> "They fear'd to brace the bow?"
> No! Celts, it never shall be, no!
>> The Gaul shall turn the day;
> Gird on the quiver, brace the bow;
>> Up! Celts, strike home and slay.'

"The chords were strong and wild as the flight of the sea-gull, and the voice deep and rolling as the blue waves it skims o'er; but oh! for the coward heart of man, these shepherds and wood-cutters, even the armed men we had trained, were moved a moment, murmured a faint applause—one or two shouting for the bard, and crying 'to arms,'—and then sank back into their old fears.

" 'What can we do against the Romans?' cried one.

" 'We have no arms, no provisions,' shouted another.

" 'No discipline,' sneered a third.

" 'We shall go out to be cut to pieces,' murmured a shepherd.

" 'Like calves in the shambles,' cried a cowardly cowherd.

" 'And our hills are better defences than our arms.'

"So they went on, while we were quiet. I was trembling in every limb. The people were before me, still obstinate, still immoveable, and if they held out, if they still refused, then not our glory, and honour only were gone, but our land, our freedom, all that we loved. I trembled, for the will of a whole people is a dire antagonist for one man. But I felt power in myself. I despised the illiterate mob. All I feared was the stubbornness of the mass, in which each clown supported his brother blockhead. Should I speak to them again, and in a tone of authority? should I, if it were necessary, even invent some message from Heaven, some divine inspiration of Bhelen? I looked instinctively towards those blue eyes of Dona for an answer. But they were no longer turned towards me. She was looking indignantly, almost angrily around her. I could see her bosom heaving yet more rapidly, her eyes gliding continually from one to another, her hand nervously drawing the long brown tresses from her brow.

"For a moment there was another awful stillness. The crowd seemed still to hesitate; still to look for somebody to reassure them. I should have sprung up then, I should have caught them in the nick of time, but all my thought, all my soul was riveted on that lovely face, working with all the passion of indignant shame.

"Suddenly I saw her stretch her arm beside her, still looking forward, and grasp a battle-axe that lay neglected by her side. One second I saw her rise, proud, furious, carried away,—the next and she had mounted beside me, and was flourishing the glittering axe above her head, with all the strength of her woman's arm.

" 'Cowards,' she cried, throwing back her fine head, and gasping with emotion. 'Cowards, for I cannot call you men: a woman shall put you to shame, a woman shall do what no warrior amongst you dares. Cowards to-day, you were not so once. What shall your fathers say in the Heaven of Bhelen? Shall your dead mothers own that they have suckled dastards? Shame, shame. I have seen the Roman, and I fear him not. I will march on to meet him; with this axe, this woman's hand, I will strike the first blow for my country, and let him follow who dares.'

"She flung the axe once more round her head, and as she did so a thousand voices leapt up, 'We will, we will! lead us on!'

"Her beauty had done what all my eloquence had not done. Her weakness, her woman's courage had shamed the young men. The older ones followed in the wake. She leapt down from the stone, and walked stately as a queen through the opening crowd. The young men clutched their weapons, and pushed forward after her. Shouting and shouting, they formed in rank. I pressed my father's hand, I called on the other Druids to follow me, and rushing on one with another, we closed behind her, and with one voice raised the war-chant of Bhelen.

" 'On! on!' she cried, in shrill accents, that rang above our hundred voices. The impulse was given. With one accord all closed behind her. Children and wives were greeted with hurried kisses; we turned with one accord, and with one voice bade adieu to the old and the feeble, and our own loved homes, and then marched rapidly from the town. The women followed us for a long way. Dona still marched at our head, waving us forward with her white arm, and her dark tresses floating in the air. On, on, with tears and cries and hopes all mingled around us, on, on, for half-an-hour across the hills, and then all again was silent. We marched steadily to death or victory.

"Three days we travelled onwards to meet the awful foe. Three nights we camped beneath the starry heaven, gathering our food from the villages we passed, and joined at every step by fresher hearts and stouter arms. Three days Dona still marched at our head, adored by all, our woman-general, stronger in her will and her ambition than any of us.

"The third night we camped behind a range of low hills, with the Roman, unconscious, in fancied security, in the valley on the other side.

"None slept. All knew that ere morning the fatal hour would come. All thought of their wives, their children, their sisters, their fathers, and their homes, that they had left. And amid all that throng, Dona was the only woman.

"Three hours after midnight the word passed in silence to prepare.

"Then there was a slight noise in the camp, if camp it could be called, with nought but bushes for our tents. The bowman was seeing to his lock and the buckle of his quiver; the woodcutter felt the edge of his axe, and sharpened it stealthily on the nearest stone; the trained warrior girded on his glaive, and took his buckler of hide on the left arm. And amid the stealthy business a light footstep woke me from thought, and Dona stood by my side.

" 'Friend,' she said to me, more warmly than she had ever spoken, 'Friend, *you* are to win the fight. To you the honour of rousing the Roman.'

"I looked in wonder at her. I, a Druid, to wield the sword?

" 'Yes,' she answered to my look. 'The frighted eagle soars not straight towards the sun, but flutters his huge pinions till the huntsman's aim is taken. Up, friend, take a Druid band with you, climb yon ridge, and wait in long line till the first beams of morning gild the hill-tops. Then with one throat pour out the war-hymn. I will do the rest.'

"I would have seized her hand, I would have fallen and worshipped her as a heroine worthy of Nehallenia's court,—but she was gone, and in silence I led my band up the heather.

"We had scarcely formed, when the first grey light twinkled in the east. In a minute or two we could see the sleeping camp beneath us, and hear the heavy footfalls of the nightwatch.

"Clothed all in white, and stretched along the ridge of the dark hill, we were a strange sight in that early morning.

"Then a long, low cry from behind was the signal. I raised my hand, and a hundred hill-trained throats poured out the wild hymn, while Cervorix, the bard, struck the ringing chords.

"A clatter in the valley; the night-guards moving rapidly, a trumpet call, a rush to arms, and the next moment the glitter of a brandished axe on a distant hill-top, the white robe of a maiden fluttering in the chill morning breeze, dark bands closing rapidly after it, and then, still in doubtful silence, a downward rush upon the foe.

"For one second we heard nothing but the clatter of arms down the distant hill, the next, a huge, wild shout that rent the air, the next, the din of close, bloody strife. We saw nothing but a huge black mass, moving unsteadily in the dark valley, but we heard the terrible cries, the axe shivering the helmet, the arrows rattling like hail upon the armour, the shouts of vengeance, hatred, wounds, death, all mingled.

"I understood it all. We had been placed there to divert attention, and our warriors had thus secured the flank attack.

"Wild with excitement, I could not endure our stillness. I bounded almost headlong from rock to rock, and rushed shouting and throwing up my arms into the fight. Everywhere the Roman, utterly surprised, was yielding ground, crying quarter, or being struck to the earth. Everywhere the axe of the Briton glittered above the invader, and everywhere I thought I saw the white robe of the warrior-maiden.

"That was my real lure. I thought fearfully of her danger, and dreamed wildly of saving her, and I rushed madly to where the white robe glittered. I saw her—saw her turn, followed her. A band of some twenty of my countrymen had surrounded three or four Southrons, who were fighting desperately with the sword. The tallest of them was cutting down his assailants right and left. I saw Dona pass her hand across her brow. I saw her waver a moment, and in that moment I saw an axe gleam above the head of the Roman knight. The next, and Dona had struck its bearer to the ground.

"The Roman stepped back at the sight of his deliverer. She swung her axe wildly round and cleared the space about him.

" 'Away, away!' she cried furiously. 'Go, Celts, and drive your foes down elsewhere. This man is my prisoner.'

"The assailants shrank back amazed, and Dona turned to the Roman and stretched her white hand to his arm.

" 'You saved me once,' she said, 'and now I save your life in quittance of my debt. That done, I am still your foe, and I claim you as my prisoner.'

"The Roman stooped. I bounded forward in my agony, and caught his words, 'Lady, your captive would I ever be.'

"Caesar recalled his forces into winter quarters. The war had ended that summer with his defeat, and the Roman soldier blushed to hear that a woman had been the general in his rout. Half the legion had been cut to pieces; the other half had either fled or been taken.

"The Roman warrior lay wounded and captive in the home of Dona's mother, and I,—I, who had hoped against hope itself, roamed, more deeply wounded in my love, pierced to the heart, and fostering yellow jealousy in my bosom.

"To Dona I never went—how could I?

"To the gods, to the temple, I went as a sneak. I felt that my heart was not with them. I shunned the mild gaze of my old father, I hated the honours that the people poured upon me. I was the most popular Druid in all the country. They coupled my name with Dona's as their deliverer. All said that the song of the Druids had saved the land. But I felt like a fiend at their praises, and when they praised Dona I rejoiced with a bitter joy.

"Over the wild hills of heather, through the thick, dark forests, I roamed half-mad. The image of my beloved one grew brighter and brighter, as I dwelt upon it. She was far more beautiful, far more a heroine—nay, she was scarcely a woman, she must be some goddess. And that *her* heart, hers, the deliverer of her race, should be given to its direst foe! Oh! it was terrible.

"But the dark night of the forest blackened my darkening soul. First came the thought of ambition. I was already a great man. I would be the greatest in the kingdom. I was a Druid—I would be a warrior too. I would take the sword and the field against the Roman, and rival Vercingetorix himself. She loved honour and glory. These would I gain. But the winter came apace. There was no fighting the Roman then; and in the frozen glades, and the deep snow, my jealous love was all that burned.

"Then it was that in despair I bethought me of slaying the southern knight. If he were once away, she might sorrow awhile, but her love would die with its object.

"Through the long, cold winter I cherished this thought. Scheme after scheme passed through my heated brain. I tutored myself to cruelty. I grew exacting and harsh to the people, who yet seemed to love me all the more. It was the business of the Arch-Druid to decide all the difficult points of quarrel between the people. He was the chief magistrate, and held the appeal from the petty chieftains.

"I became my father's adviser, and privily urged him to punishments of intense cruelty, which the old man abhorred in his soul, but in which he yielded to my stronger will. Thus I became a tyrant.

"Meanwhile my father was building this temple in which you lie. He had been about it for a year. The stones were graven with the mystic signs; the cave was dug out slowly. It was nearing its completion, and when the first spring sun turned the frosts to water, the work was recommenced.

"One day he begged me to go and see the first stones placed against the walls. I came to Gavr Inis, and when my work was done I strolled down the island, drawn by an irresistible impulse towards the cottage of Dona.

"As I trod the wet rotting leaves of the oak forest, I caught the sound of coming footsteps. Instinctively I hid myself in the hollow of an oak. On they came, and then from my lurking place I saw the Roman Knight circling his stout arm around Dona's gentle form. I felt my brows meet, I felt my breath choking me, I felt the hot blood rush into my head, as they passed. I longed to dart out and strangle him with these hands, but a spirit within me muttered, 'Wait.'

"They came, each pouring love into the other's lips; and Dona, she I loved and longed for, gazing into his eyes with burning passion. And thus they passed, and I held back my vengeance.

"The spring came, and again the land was roused. The Roman was alive again, and again his dreaded arms were turning to the west. All were mad with fear. They sought Dona, and implored her to lead them on again, and she only shook her head, and said nought. They sought me, and I assembled the people.

"My dreadful purpose was made up.

" 'Celts,' I cried to the assembly, 'the gods are wroth with us. Our faith is tottering, our temples are deserted, our sacrifices are not what they once were, and for this Bhelen sends the Roman upon our land. If you would be saved you must make one grand propitiation.'

" 'Speak, speak,' cried a hundred voices, 'we are ready to do anything. Our cattle, our flocks, are Bhelen's. Let the god command.'

" 'No,' I answered, smiling bitterly, 'the blood of oxen and the blood of sheep are stale to the offended god. Think you a common offering can appease him? No. Last night I stood beneath Bhelen's holy oak, and whispered my prayer in the bark. The leaves fluttered, and they answered me. 'A man, a man,' was the oracle. 'One man must die for the many.'

"The people and the chieftains, and the Druids, all stood aghast. How long had it been since a man had been slain in sacrifice? Never since the days of their grandsires.

" 'Yes,' I cried again, 'ye are fostering in your very bosom an enemy of our land and our gods. A Roman dwells among us in safety, and a Roman is an insult to the Holy Bhelen.'

"The assembly breathed again. All knew who was meant, and now none feared for himself.

" 'It is good,' they cried, 'the offering shall be made.'

"I turned to my father, who stood pale and trembling—not with age, but horror—at my side.

" 'Father,' I said, 'your new temple is all but finished. This will be fine blood to hallow it, better than that of bulls and goats.'

" 'Horrible, horrible,' muttered the old man, turning from me in disgust, 'and that Bhelen should have asked for human blood!'

" 'And yet,' I answered humbly, 'it is Bhelen's will, father; it must be done.'

"He said nothing, but hurried away.

"I passed a horrible night. My father's disgust at me—he, always so fond, so proud of his son,—had struck me deeply, and now set me thinking. I now saw that my last friend had been undeceived in me. One by one my links to life had dropped away. There seemed to be no hope of Dona's love, which had once been the constant companion of my mind. Though I dreamed at times of such a hope, though that was the excuse I made to my own conscience for the deed I was preparing to do, I knew well that there was really none. Then the people too had found me out. I had tyrannised, I had become brutal, and though they respected my talents, and the divine communications which I pretended were made to me, there was not one who loved me—not one. And now even my father seemed to loathe my cruelty, for this last act was dreadful.

"I confess that for a moment I was weak, when these thoughts oppressed me; for a moment I wavered. I said to myself, 'What right hast thou to this man's blood? Why shouldst thou hate him for an accident. He does not even dream that he has a rival. Thou hast no right even to be his rival, for thou hast never told thy love. What! wilt thou make these two wretched that are now so happy? Thou yearnest thyself for Love, for something on which to lean thy soul, as a head on the pillow. Thou yearnest for some soft beauty to rest thy cheek on her warm breast, that thou mayest gaze up into her eyes for sympathy, and feel her bosom heaving in her love. Thou longest for all this, and thou knowest that they have found it. Canst thou be so cruel, so remorseless as to tear them from this joy?'

"But then as I raised to myself this picture of perfect Love, that other picture which I had seen from the hollow of the oak flashed back upon me. It was a demon's doing, and I writhed with hatred, with wounded self-love.

" 'I will not only have his blood,' I cried, 'but I will make her— yes *her*, take it. He shall die by the white hand that fondles him.'

"The resolution was grand, and I spent a night of heat and fury, tossing on my bed of hide and straw, and planning the affair.

"I rose a little before the sun, and bent my steps in the direction of a distant village, called Cœr-Brachd. Once arrived there, I marched straight to the house of a Druid whom I knew.

" 'Friend,' I said, when the ordinary greetings were over, 'you have two Roman prisoners among your slaves; you find them troublesome, I hear, and difficult to bring to work. Say what value you put upon them and I will give it you.'

"The Druid clasped my hand.

" 'Last night,' he said hurriedly, 'the news came here from Cœr-Bhelen, that some Roman prisoner was to be sacrificed. These men heard it, and fearful lest the lot should fall on them, they attempted to escape for the ninth time this winter, but my trusty Britons again foiled their essay. But you see how I am troubled with them. Besides, they refuse to draw water or hew wood. I would far sooner have some dozen sheep, or a new set of arms for my men.'

" 'You shall have both,' I said.

"He called a witness, who brought a javelin, which I broke on my knee, as a sign of a firm contract.

"An hour after my Romans were receiving their lesson from

me. I told them that the people had demanded the blood of the Roman Knight, and that I, for my own reasons, and for friendship's sake, was willing to save him; that I had bought them up for the purpose of aiding me, and that if they did my bidding their liberty was secure, but not otherwise.

"The night before had been very stormy, and the wind was still blowing furiously. It was very early too, and so I felt certain that the news of my assembly had not yet reached Gavr Inis. I therefore took my own boat, spread the red sail, and carried the two Romans privily over.

"I fixed a trysting place for them in the forest near Wenedh, and sent them to Dona herself. They were to tell her that the people had resolved to slay her lover in sacrifice, but that *I*—I whom she had always respected, who was ever her friend, had thus schemed to save the Knight and the man she was affianced to. I could not doubt that Dona would at once relinquish her prisoner.

"I landed them at Gavr Inis, and sped back in my bark to Cœr-Bhelen. Here I rushed madly along the street, calling loudly for help. The people poured from their houses in sad alarm.

" 'This morn,' I cried, 'I went to Cœr-Brachd, and bought two Roman slaves of the Druid Grosna. I wished that they too should be led in triumph to the sacrifice of propitiation, and be humbled by the sight of their Knight's slaughter. It seems that they had learnt our intention, and as we came along by the water's edge they saw my boat. Suddenly one of them seized me by the neck, threw me down, and held me there by the throat, while the other jumped into the skiff and spread the sail; then the first leapt up and jumped into the boat after his companion, before I could prevent it, and I saw them steer their way to the forest of Wenedh. Up friends and after them, seek them in the forest and bring them back, for if they escape they will reveal all to the Romans, and we are lost. Meanwhile I will go and secure the other on Gavr Inis.'

"A score of stout forms sprang into their boats, and some five or six sails were soon wafting them across the sea.

"I stretched my hide towards Gavr Inis, for I knew that they would take much longer to reach the forest than I should to gain the island. Like a wild horse, I bounded through the oaken groves on the island, and when I reached Dona's hut the two Romans were just preparing the boat, and Dona and the Knight were standing on the shore.

"'No,' I heard her cry from my hiding-place, 'no, I will not weep. It is better that you should go alone, without me, and yet I seem to fear some mishap. But what matter? you are fleeing from a frightful death here, and in the forest and across the hills you will have to meet, at worst, a foe that you can combat. Now I will bind on your sword, and for my sake use it nobly.'

"She stooped, took up his sword, which was lying beside him, and girt it round his hips.

"'Yes,' she continued, 'I shall follow you. You will await me in the forest, and ere sundown I shall see you again—and then no longer a captive, but a free citizen of hateful Rome. Yes, for I do hate Rome—and love it too—for your sake. But you will re-member your vow—you will turn the Roman from our land. You will tell them how barren, how wretched it is. But ah! I shall be with you then—and yet—'

"She threw her arms around his neck, and hung upon his lips, and I exulted in my awful secret, for I knew that that embrace was the last.

"He tore himself away, and leapt into the boat. And she stood with clasped hands upon the beach, and I could see that she was pressing down her tears.

"The boat dashed wildly over the foam, and was borne away farther and farther. Still she stood and watched it, till the red sail was but a speck between heaven and the ocean. Then she fell upon her knees, and threw her hands to heaven, and the hot tears rolled in a torrent down her pale, pale cheeks.

"She rose again, and looked in vain for the distant boat. Then, dashing her hand across her eyes, she turned into the hut, slowly and sorrowfully. At that moment my heart smote me. I longed to spring to her side, to tell her all—to bid her despise me—to res-cue her lover, and to undo my wretched deed. But this time, the demon within me was stronger still, and I nestled in my own hatred.

"She came out again, with a large grey woollen cloak over her shoulders. I watched her set the sail of her little skiff; and then, bounding back through the forest, I steered my own towards the wood of Wenedh.

"I followed her at some distance for a time, and then turning the helm, reached another part of the mainland, and made for the trysting-place. I saw that she had steered round an island which was in the way, and that she could not reach the shore till some time after me.

"The forest of Wenedh was cut about with paths and ox-tracks in different directions, but all met at one spot. It was there that I had appointed the trysting-place. I mounted the wooded steeps rapidly, and turning, after a time, I saw, through an open glen, the distant sea, and the five sails of the pursuers spread towards Cœr-Bhelen. Was he among them?

"I sped on, and reached the trysting-place. I saw the marks of a skirmish. I traced them over the rotting leaves, and presently came upon the body of one of the Romans, lying dead in a pool of blood. A little farther on the other was pinioned to a tree by a javelin.

"In a moment my plans were formed. I carried both the bodies to a distance, and covered them with brushwood and dry leaves.

"Then I returned to the trysting-place and sat down.

"In a few minutes I heard a rustling behind me. Though I knew it was Dona, I started like a guilty thief. She was coming on quickly and hopefully. The moment she saw me, she rushed towards me.

" 'Where is he?' she cried, 'Oh! tell me where he is.'

"I looked up with a face of well-feigned grief. I exulted in this moment of triumph.

" 'Dona,' I said, 'sit down, while I tell you all.'

" 'Is he alive? is he safe? Tell me, tell me.'

" 'Patience,' I answered, 'Listen to me, and you shall hear where he is. You know my hopes of saving him. You know that I brought the two Romans to Gavr Inis—'

" 'Yes, yes, but tell me all.'

" 'I will. But listen. I sailed back when I had landed them. I found Cœr-Bhelen in an uproar. I was surrounded, threatened—'

" 'And you betrayed him?' She looked at me with eyes of hate.

" 'No, no, never. They had seen me leave the shore with the Romans. They accused me of a plot to release the knight. I denied all—everything. I told them that the two Romans had gone straight to Wenedh, for I thought to put them off the track, and I sailed hastily back to Gavr Inis, to stop the—the—your lover—Dona—'

" 'Yes, yes—my beloved—'

" 'From going to the forest. But they must have discovered all. I sailed once more from Gavr Inis to the forest, still hoping to warn the fugitives, and as I touched the shore I met their pursuers coming back with three bodies borne among them, which they threw into the sea. The knight was one of them.'

"Her expression had changed, as I spoke, from anxiety to a fearful calm. She looked me sternly in the face, as a lioness might look, and I could not meet her eyes.

" 'You lie,' she said, calmly and firmly. 'You lie, he cannot be dead.'

" 'Would to heaven I lied,' I answered, with tears in my voice—sham tears. 'Follow me and I will show you.'

"I broke through the brushwood, and she followed to the spot where I had found the first body.

" 'That is his blood,' I said, pointing to the red pool.

" '*His* blood?'

"She gathered herself together, her eyes turned up, then closed, and with a long loud shriek, she threw herself into the pool of gore.

"I stood above her, laughing in my sleeve at her credulity, laughing at the pangs, which I had power to inflict, and did inflict. It was better this—than bullying peasants, or wringing the innocent with tortures. It was a keener, more intellectual pleasure. But still I feared I felt what did not amount to trembling, but had all the pain of a guilty horror.

"Then I sat down on a ledge of stone, and coolly watched her. The grey cloak had half slipt off, and left her white shoulders bare. I saw that their whiteness now was not that of healthful beauty, but a bloodless pallor. Once or twice I saw the flesh quiver, as she lay with her face on the ground, and seemed to kiss what she believed was his blood.

"I sat for at least half-an-hour, while she remained motionless.

"I did not care now to go after my other captive. This enjoyment was enough for the day, and I revelled in the imagination of what her thoughts must be as she lay there; if, at least, she did think, but perhaps she had swooned. I cared not, but I watched her till the setting sun reminded me of the evening chill, which I had not felt till then.

"Beyond her form the hill shelved rapidly down, and the pines, those sombre giants, who alone seemed to favour this gloomy spot, stretched up in tall, thin ranks, with leaves and brushwood crowding round their feet. Far, far behind them, I could catch a glimpse of the ocean, and the slant rays were gilding the alternate leaves, and now played fitfully on my victim at my feet.

"But dark clouds gathered round the sun, and the shadows seemed to close me in behind. I felt frightened at my own wickedness, I shuddered, got up, and touched Dona's arm.

" 'Dona.' I spoke in a tone of well-feigned sympathy.

"She did not move, nor answer. I circled her waist with my arm, and raised her up. The drops of blood fell off her face and bosom, and she stood up before me—changed—utterly changed; and yet she had not shed a single tear. Gently, almost imperceptibly, she glided from my grasp,—a grasp in which there was no guilty longing—and turning her pale face, covered with the cold blood, from me, stretched me her hand.

" 'Thank you, thank you,' she said, in a hoarse low whisper. 'Thank you for all you have done, or wished to do. Now, leave me.'

" 'No, Dona,' I answered, still in a voice full of false tears, 'I may not leave you here. You know the Briton well. You know his vengeance, and his thirst of blood. Now, that they have slain the knight—'

"She trembled visibly.

" 'They will seek you. You must not return to Gavr Inis. They will devour you.'

" 'And what matter, if they do?' she said, calmly, and drew her hand across her brow.

" 'It must not be. You would not tempt these dogs to another murder.' She was silent, and again trembled slightly.

" 'I know your heart too well. Besides, remember your mother.' She uttered a bitter 'Ah!'

" 'I will secure her. I will secure you too. There is a hut at the border of the forest, far from Wenedh, far from Gavr Inis, where you must remain a day or two, till all is calm again, till these blood-lappers have forgotten the murder of your lover.'

"How I delighted to remind her of that! But this time she betrayed no feeling of it.

" 'I will lead you there now, and to-morrow I will come to you, give you news of your mother, and hopes for the future. There is an old woman at the hut, who will take good care of you. Come.'

"Still she did not move. She was looking down at the blood on the ground.

" 'Come,' I repeated, taking her arm in my hand, 'the sun is down. Ere long the night will come on, and the wolf will steal from his lair. Come, Dona.'

"She walked passively beside me, but still she turned her face away. Presently we passed a running stream. She stopped, and thought a moment. Then stooping down, she washed the blood from her face and robe, looked silently up to heaven, and then followed me.

"The old woman was a hag, who lived alone and watched the stars. I drew her aside, promised her two sheep, and told her to be kind to her charge, but never leave her side for a moment.

" 'Three days hence,' I said to her, 'a woodcutter will come to the house and ask for food. Give him some, and talk to him. He will tell you that the Romans have had a battle with some of the chieftains. That they are marching this way. That two or three prisoners have been taken and brought to Cœr-Bhelen, and that all the folk are in terror. It will be a lie, mother, but you must believe it, and take care that the maiden hears it.'

"I left them, and returned across the sea to Cœr-Bhelen.

"I found the people in high glee. They had had a fight for their prisoner, killed the two Romans and captured the knight.

" 'Good,' I said, 'in seven days he shall be offered to Bhelen.'

"I visited my prisoner, but only once. There was so deep a reproach to me in his quiet, contemptuous smile, that I could not triumph over him, if indeed my mind had been vulgar enough to do so. But it was not. My triumph was in my own heart. I exulted in causing misery where I could not myself enjoy. Besides these cruelties were grown a habit, at least in mind.

"The knight did not thank me. Probably he suspected me, knowing more of man's villainy than poor Dona did. On my side I took no trouble to explain anything. I came there simply to tell him that he was destined to replace the ox and the ram at the sacrifice, and to enjoy his horror at the news.

"He turned very pale for a moment, and then I noticed a kind of swallowing in his throat, as he said, 'Sir, a Roman citizen can always die.'

"I left him in his chains, and sailed again across to the opposite shore. Dona had lain upon the straw, so the hag told me, but had not seemed to sleep. In the morning she had refused all food, and sat at the door, looking at the forest near at hand.

"I was very kind to her in my mockery. I talked to her about becoming a Druidess, about dedicating her virgin form to Nehallenia. She seemed to listen, but said nothing.

"Day after day I went. I persuaded a wood-cutter to play the part I had arranged, and the same day I rushed breathless into the hut, to confirm the false news. I added that some prisoners had been taken, and that the people had decided on a human sacrifice.

"She only shuddered.

"The next day I came to tell her that the people were calling for her. That they protested she alone was fit to strike the blow; that Bhelen had revealed to me in the quivering of the oak-leaves that no sacrifice would be accepted, unless a warrior maiden slew the victim.

"Her fixed eyes turned to me for the first time, and looked through me, till I trembled beneath them. But I made a grand effort. I rose, still answering her gaze, and said, 'What Bhelen bids us, no one dare refuse.'

"Then for the first time she spoke.

" 'Will Bhelen save the Land if this is done?'"

" 'He will.'

" 'Then I will do it. I am ready.'

"I was myself again. The next two days I passed in preparing the procession.

"On the night of the third day, a mighty crowd was brought together on Gavr Inis. The stars were bright and numberless. The sky was moonless and doubly blue.

"A wild air thrilled along the branches of the oaks; and three bards, with Cervorix at their head, trod slowly up towards this temple.

"They were followed by a band of maidens, and Dona led them, holding in her falling arm a bright, sharp dagger. The music thrilled again wild and melancholy, and voices caught it up behind. A hundred white-clad Druids, their brows wreathed with oak-leaves, and branches of the ash in their hands, chanted the hymn of penitence. Then came two figures. Over one was thrown a long white cloth, that covered his head, and hid his naked body. This was the victim, and I led him by the hand.

"My father followed, with his silvery locks bent down as if in shame. And last, a band of Druidesses bore the glittering torches, streaming in the light breeze, and glaring on the ghost-like trunks of the huge oaks. The warriors and the people followed in a motley crowd.

"At the foot of the hill the long train stopped and turned. All were at last assembled, and as I came up, I saw Dona, calm, white as death, but yet with a look of quiet contentment on her sunken face. I saw her turn a glance full of pity at my victim, but it was clear she suspected nothing, and I had so arranged that she arrived only at the moment of the procession setting off; and as it was forbidden to speak when once it had begun, she could scarcely have discovered who the victim really was. She seemed to be happy again for a moment in the hope of saving her people, for in this strange being the love of her country seemed stronger than even that other love.

"The whole mass knelt at the foot of the hill. Here at least was true grief; the Roman was coming, and they knelt in real fear, real prayer for their hearths and homes. The bards mounted to midway up the hill, and Cervorix, strange bard, sang again.

'An eaglet's blood shall stain his hand,
    A woman lead the host,
A maiden's death-shriek fill the land,
    And the Druid's rule be lost.'

"I trembled as the words swam down clear and ringing into my very brain. I had counted for all this, but still I trembled.

"Then regaining my firmness in the strength of my hatred, I led the victim up the hill. Dona followed near, but now alone. Behind her came my father, stooping, sinking more than ever. One Druid bore the vase to catch his blood, another bore a torch, and that was all.

"My father turned midway and blessed the kneeling people. At last we entered the low mouth of the temple. The two Druids marched first, and I thanked the darkness that covered at last my guilty pallor. I passed behind the smoking torch, still holding the prisoner's hand. Dona was next, and my tottering father came slowly, last.

"In the temple all knelt, but my victim and I. I took a cord from the hand of one of the Druids, turned the knight's back to this hole that you see, and taking his hands, bound them firmly to this shaft. Then I drew the ends of the white cloth over his shoulders, laying bare his hairy chest, but not his head.

"I looked at Dona, as I did so. She was bowed in fervent prayer.

"Then my father rose, and in a smothered voice, and raising his hands to heaven, he murmured:—'Oh! wrathful God, Oh! mighty formless Bhelen, will this appease thee? Oh! wash our sins out with this Roman blood.'

"The knight was motionless still. Then the torch-bearer drew near. The other Druid came to the left of the victim, and held his vase beneath the heart. I stood at the right, holding with my hands the ends of the white cloth that covered him.

"Then I motioned to Dona to draw near. She rose, she sighed slightly, and stood before the victim. She raised the dagger, with the point to his heart. Again I motioned with my head. She cried,

" 'I strike for my people.'

"I felt the victim start, I heard him cry bitterly 'Dona,' as he caught her voice. I quivered, for I thought all was lost, but the same instant I saw the blood spurt from his heart, and jerked the cloth from his head.

"Dona had started back. She had seized the torch from the Druid's hand, she had passed it before the dead man's face, her eyes starting from their sockets, her hair streaming wildly behind. She had thrown the torch down again, she glared fearfully into the victim's face, she passed her thin hands across his brow, parted his hair asunder, and even while I looked at her with bitter exultation, snatched the dagger from his heart, and with a fierce, long, awful shriek that shook the very stones, plunged it reeking into her own. I fled."

"And what did you do?" I asked, when the terrible scene was over. "Whither did you flee?"

"To the Romans," he muttered. "I became their spy, and led them to devour my own father's house. Stay, —"

He laid his heavy hand on my shoulder. I started, for I knew it was a murderer's. I jumped up, and as I did so, a bluff harsh voice at my side, cried: "Monsieur must get up. This wind won't last, and we had better be off before it changes."

I rubbed my eyes. The old sailor of last night was before me. The daylight was struggling dimly into the cave, and I saw clearly that he was not a Druid. I also noticed that my nether garments lay just in the place where the Druid had thrown himself on his face, and that they now caught the stray beam of day, and looked white.

I rubbed my eyes again and looked round the temple.

"Come, sir," said the sailor, in a hurry, "my wife will be tired of waiting for me. Have you had a good night?"

"Pretty well," I answered, as I gazed round the strange place. "I must have dreamed a good deal."

"Perhaps it was not all dreaming, sir," replied the other, doubtfully.

"By the way," I said as we were getting into the boat, "I heard some strange music last night. Were you singing?"

The two sailors looked blank at one another. "We heard it too," said the younger one, rather pale, "and thought it was Monsieur."

The boat dashed over the waves, and I lay in the bottom, thinking of Dona and the Druid. At last the keel grated on the shingle.

"Already at Cœr-Bhelen?" I cried, jumping up.

"Cœr-Bhelen!" answered the sailors, staring at one another in amazement. "This is Locmariaquer." "Ah," rejoined the elder one, "Monsieur *has* seen the man in white, then."

The Cousins

By Edward Burne-Jones

The dancers swept merrily by me on that night of Lady Lacy's ball eleven years ago, and fanned me pleasantly as they bounded past to the tune of instruments, and there was nothing in all this to make me peevish, and fretful, and morose; yet I stood aside moodily, taking no part in the dancing, nor the talk—and though I asked myself often how it was that I felt so evil-minded on that night, yet I needed no answer, knowing well the reason, that it was because of my cousin Gertrude, and her troop of flatterers, and because she slighted me openly, putting me to shame before all who knew our betrothal; and because I could not help thinking that somehow her love had grown cold of late. And some there were who rated me for my gloomy looks, and pestered me with silly questionings, to which I lent little heed or answer. And all the while Gertrude was hidden from me by a ring of satellites, but her silver laugh and jesting troubled me heavily. "To-morrow," said I, "I will speak to her kindly and firmly, and if it must be so, release her whatever comes to me." I had fancied moreover that her father's manner was shy and altered to me when I crossed him in the Hall; for he passed by me with unwonted coldness, and left the house immediately. Two gentlemen were talking in a low tone to one another, close at hand, but, though I moved to be out of overhearing, I had unconsciously caught the substance of their conversation, earnest and grave—some great failures in the north had followed the strikes, and certain great city houses were said to be deeply involved in the loss. Why should I, with unreasoning, overleaping thought, so swiftly couple this with that strange meeting in the hall? I cannot tell, only a fear not wholly indefinite fell upon me.

I would leave now; where was the hostess, my firm, most constant protector in all boyish scrapes? In the glance I gave round the room I saw that Gertrude was not there: I was at her ladyship's side presently, and held out my hand. "So soon, Charlie, you must be ill; upon my word you look so, let me"—"No, dear Lady Lacy, there is positively nothing the matter with me, a slight headache perhaps"; and as I urged this it came upon me indeed quick and throbbing—"my father said he should want me at a very early hour in the morning, and I cannot fail him." "It is not much past twelve," she said; "you are not generally so particular about sleep. Poor boy!" I saw she was aware of more than she expressed. A kind look and kinder pressure. "I am sorry I prepared such an entertainment for you, Charlie; good bye."

Yet I could not go without saying "good-night" to my beautiful cousin, who caused me such secret sorrow, but knew it not. Passing the refreshment room I saw her, as I thought, sitting in the cool, for her face was scarlet with the flush of dancing, and slightly bent, but another step discovered that she was not alone, and what I saw besides I say not: then I passed out straightway into the night, where the snow lay deep upon the ground on that February morning, feeling not heart-broken and crushed as I used to think I should feel, if any great distress fell upon me, but full of animal spirit and strange excitement. There was not a star in all the sky: I was glad there were none to look down with their far-off, cold and restless eyes upon me; but a thick covering of snow-cloud was wrapped about the earth and shrouded it all night long. As I stepped upon the pavement the half-clothed, shivering form of a woman came and cried to me. "Pity, oh! pity, it is so cold, and my child is starving, Sir—no home, nor food for it all this day long"; and all her voice was broken by the chattering of her set teeth in the frozen jaws. Surely, surely it was the good Lord sent this encounter, at the moment when my selfish heart was thinking only of its grief; for when the woman was gone, a deep shame and inward silence came upon me, such, only stronger according to the growth of years, as in younger days had smitten me with cruel contrast when a lean starved face pressed itself into silly flatness against a pastry-cook's window, when I was within. Contrast, why contrast then? did I not indeed know that every day misery walked the gay streets with opulence, and squalor shared the houses with fashion? Ah! but man is very brave in the sunlight—did one ever behold a wraith in the noon-day, or see meridian glamour? but the hour and waste of darkness, how are they not phantomed with infinite spirits!

"No home, no food all the day long," and yet our dogs are housed and fed! Oh! there should be echo of these words, reverberation deep and hollow, through every happy home at midnight, when the lights are out, and all men are at once alone,—"No home"; "no food." Is it true? Question the winds that blow over cities at night-time, what voices they bear along with them. Is it enough, oh! good people, to thank God night and morning for home and life?—will it be asked ever at any time, chiefly at one great time, "Where is thy brother?"—will it be answered, "Am I my brother's keeper?"

Alas! poor heart of mine how should I ever comfort it again! already I was changed, even in this brief time. I said within myself, "Since no good sleep can come to me this night, I will walk among the streets till morning, and see the woe of the great city"—and while the words were yet within my mind, I struck upon it unawares.

"Oh! Richard—Dickey, doan't—mercy! you'll hurt the child —oh!"—God! the cry that went up shrieking to thy heaven—oh! didst Thou hear it? yet there came down no thunder nor fire, nor did the ground beneath open and consume. She had gone down before that fearful blow, her poor head striking, as it fell, against the projecting window-frame—surely she is dead: three or four men came out of the tap-room at the cry, for it was keen and piercing. I saw that they were drunk, all of them, like the monster who had done this evil deed; he stood leaning against the wall, all unconscious, muttering curses. I was kneeling upon the snow beside her now; it was a cruel sight beneath the wretched glimmer of the lamp-light—her cheek and mouth were full of blood; as I raised her head it flowed over me; presently I think she would have choked in the swoon: her bonnet fell from her to the ground as I lifted her, and her hair, wet with the trampled snow, was long and raven black. I took no heed to the inarticulate gabble round me; I knew the wretch had staggered towards me, making the dark air black with oaths, that his silly, half-witted comrades were doing their feeble best to lead him back, and once my arm received a kick meant for the helpless form it shielded:—but my eyes were upon her countenance trying to trace below the signs of want and famine, the lines of what must once have been tender, well-nigh beautiful.

The noise of the sliding and staggering of their feet was stopped by the swinging to of the door. I followed the direction of her arm to reach the pulse; the hand was very firmly clasping something—both hands; surely not a child, not a child?

"Wot's up 'ere, Sir?—a woman drunk I s'pose."

"Oh! policeman, look down here—look at this child." He stooped and disengaged it tenderly enough for the man. "Why it's dead, sir, stone dead—but not cold yet: may be she killed it herself a-fallin." "No, no, no; the man's in there, in there, her husband, who struck her down." There was horror upon my face I know, and pride of experience in his voice as he answered, "Why, bless yer, sir, these things 'appens plenty enough; every night pretty nigh." "See her looked to and sheltered for the night, and from the brute in there." Then I left money with him, and hurried away.

It began again to snow thickly, coming slantwise against the cheek, so that I was fain to lower my head awhile, and let the storm pass by. A dull and heavy sound of the quarters came from time to time from the churches, and at long intervals a traveller would pass rapidly, and, saving this, I seemed already alone in the great streets, yet I knew this could not be; somewhere in desolate bye-lanes I knew there was homeless woe, but a terror of the unknown evil chained me to the great thoroughfares, and I never left them.

An hour more and I was leaning against the parapet of Waterloo Bridge, where I have often stood since then, in dreams; as I have stood once in reality, by another river in another city, watching not the river nor the rush of the rough water, which lay indeed viewless far below, known only by reflection from dim lamps on bridges beyond, but watching the flow of silence and the darkness, as I could not from the narrow streets—darkness and silence infinite, most unlike that we meet on trackless moors, and on high mountain tops, but laden with the pestilence of huddled crowds, and all the untold horrors of cities. I know not what unnameable horror is borne upon this nightly silence upon bridges—some dreadful dolour, ineffable, mysterious there is in it, which makes the great bridges at that hour, to my thinking, more awful than any place on earth. Where lies the horror? have I read somewhere, years ago, when my little store of reading made fancy doubly dear, and a legend was a thing remembered, did I read a story of self-inflicted death and murder underneath the arches? Only this I know, that all weird perplexity, and strange uncertain horror, and ghastly trooping of multitudinous forms, that crowd and sway and palpitate in shifting gloom, are all, all gathered together here, so that in evil dreams, which kept me nightly company many a long year afterwards, there was, chief of all, an oppressive haunting of my confused sense by a dark swift river, cold and rough and treacherous, far below me, banked on both sides of its limitless shores by a multitude of human beings, who cast forth arms of supplication across the water, while they wept and watched and waited, looking for some deliverance that never came nor would come till the end.

So standing trancedly, gathering in great store of fearful imagination for dreams to come, there fell upon my ear a sound of confused voices from the south side as of people quarrelling, which at times grew shrill and then ceased again, and recommenced. I hurried across the bridge as fast as my feet would bear me, in the snow, towards the direction of the noise, for the inter-

vening space could not be great: turning the corner of the second street, the cries were again distinct, as if a door had suddenly
opened, close at hand now; the cries of a young girl uppermost
in wild supplication. "Oh! mother, mother, loose me, let me
go—I can't go home, loose me, let me go;" and they were answered by curses and reproaches, and names, hard and bitter. I
heard them—the most stained and spotted names that women
bear did her mother call her; and the soiled and sullied gaiety of
her. dress, and the rent and shattered comeliness of her face told
a tale, not unheard before: for a moment the girl freed herself
from the clenched and tightened hold of the other, and fled
down the street. I saw the mother's face then under the glimmer
of the misty lamp,—saw the fruitless outstretching of her bare
thin arms, and the totter forward, and the fall. I stayed not a
moment, but was in pursuit, quickly overtaking and bringing
back my poor prisoner, crying and sobbing, "Let me go, sir, for
God's sake; don't take me back again to mother." Her sobbing
was so violent that she was powerless now, and I led her gently to
the place where her mother sat, for she had risen and was sitting
on a step, moaning in a low voice, and rocking with the anguish
of her soul. And in that hour, standing with those lonely ones on
the winter morning, I was suddenly aware of a change come over
me; knew that all the joy and pleasure of life had passed in a
moment, and a new order had begun; felt a shiver pass through
every limb that the night wind had not caused; knew afterwards
it was the unsheathing of the sword for battle by the angel of my
life; and while the chill was yet upon me, the bells rang out the
hour of four, and I said within myself, "I shall never laugh again
until I die." The moment of the crisis had passed, and I was
awake again. I touched the woman on the shoulder, holding her
daughter by the hand. "She is come back to you," I said, "she will
never leave you any more; come, look up, she is waiting to be
forgiven;" but the mother never ceased to rock and sway to and
fro, muttering indistinctly, "I guessed it above a month ago,
when it kep' me awake night after night—her'd better ha' died,
like Jenny, though her was clemmed, nor come to this—hers the
last of 'em a'—her'd better ha' died, like Jenny, though I seed
her starving." There upon the snow, at the feet of her wasted

mother, did she throw herself, crying, "Mother, forgive me, I'm going home, mother; I am, indeed; I shall never leave you any more—look up, look up—there, there, now take me, hold me, mother, so, so—hush, we'll beg our way from this London tomorrow; we'll stop no more—hush—oh! my God!" A storm of sobs and broken cries, as from hearts nigh rending—then a lull of quiet weeping, face to face. I left all the contents of my purse in the daughter's hand, and drew away, lest I should break the holy peace that had not been with them since innocency fled.

Two acts of the great city tragedy that is played every night; but "enough," I said, "enough, I can bear no more horrors, for surely the worst misery is not simple homelessness, nor cold nor hunger, but something worse than all these together; oh! far worse." And remorse came upon me for all the years of my life, spent in thoughtless indifference to misery so near me, and a cowardly dread lest I should not go unpunished. I was very cold, and eyesore with the bitter wind, as I retraced my steps towards the abbey. As I passed the house which I had left five hours before, the upper windows were still a-light, and upon the drawn blinds great shadows fell at intervals. The dancing went on still: how well I knew the life that was passing there! at another time I could have laughed, fancying the little tumult of pride and passion there enacting, how little! Yet there was present to my mind then only a sense of injustice and wrong, of happiness unmerited and misery undeserved, a feeling of monstrous hard inequality that, coming with the vividness of a new emotion on my overstrained sympathy, sent me for the moment reeling down precipitate gulfs of thought, leading I knew not whither. God forgive me; yet between those walls of feasting and the outer misery was not the distance very short? even as brief, I think, as between the turf we walk upon to-day, and the coffin that shall lie below presently.

In the deep darkness of the fog I saw a carriage drive up, and by and by the form of one I knew stept out of the wide doorway, shawled close against the night air, but not to be mistaken by me; an officer, whom I also knew, discharged my duty, more gallantly, I confessed, and gracefully, than I had ever done it, bowed low, and so returned.

The morning came at length, gloomy and bringing a fall of frozen sleet, but I was glad of its coming in any form, however wretched. One by one the gas-lights were put out, and at street corners were little gatherings of men and boys, making their spare, comfortless breakfast, before the day's labour: the growth of the new morning was marked more by the increase of passing feet than of light. Rapidly I made my way homewards now; my father wanted me early, and I had never failed him; it was yet good time when I reached home, for the window-blinds were down, and the shutters still unclosed. I knocked, and as if some one were that moment at the door, it opened immediately, even before I had ceased to rap. "Why John," I said, "you haven't been sitting up and watching for me, have you?" for the old man looked ill, and shivered violently, I thought, with cold, but it was not so. "Is my father up?" Before he answered, the door of the first room in the hall opened, and our physician came forward and took me by the hand. I was speechless, because of the old man's trembling and the presence of our physician; the latter led me into the room, closed the door, and caught me by both hands. "I have melancholy news for you, Mister Charles; can you bear it? rest upon this chair a moment—your poor father is no more; he was called suddenly, very suddenly away at four this morning." I heard every word distinctly, never were my ears more wakeful; at four o'clock too. I struggled for a moment to free myself, and go to him lying dead, but my knees smote together and failed me, and I fell against the table; there followed a dizziness and confused reeling of all objects in the room, which by and by passed away, and left me weak, but not speechless. "I will go and see him now, Sir; I am strong again." A look of unutterable pity fell upon me for a moment, and from its strangeness a fearful and horrible suspicion linked itself with that foreshadowed fear of seven hours back, so that I shouted and passed out, and along the hall to the staircase foot, and fell there swooning.

When I was again conscious I found myself in my own room upon my bed, where I remained two days and nights in deep oblivion of all things. Neither in all that time did I undress or partake of any food, but lay quiet and still as they laid me, sleeping deeply nearly all the time; but in the morning of the third day, so soon as the gloaming had melted into fuller daylight through the windows, I rose and passed into my father's presence—he bade me be there early, and I came. Now ever since the Lord Christ rose from the grave upon the third day, it has not ceased to happen with the dead that all the beauty of their former days should be renewed for a little space in their countenance, more purified and cleansed than it had ever been in youth and life, and all the sin and evil passed away utterly, and after that the change, and the corruptible given to corruption. And it was so with him; for as I stood bending above his face, white as the whitest marble, I saw the features crowned with a greater beauty than they had ever had in life. There a full hour afterwards they found me, and led me away unresistingly; but in the longing and the yearning of my heart to be with him during that mysterious hour, I think I reached the limits of life and death, and was not far from overpassing. I saw him no more again. They took him from his own room, the chamber of his little hopes and schemes for me—oh! not for himself, but me— his child, who lay deeply sleeping in the chamber above his head, while he kept vigil. They took him beyond his old familiar doors once more, and down the street once more, and a silly pageant with him of black draped mockeries, and plumes that shook mournfully to one refrain of "nevermore," making my heart stone, and my head sick with close air and desolation. And I returned to the great house where we had all lived once, my mother, and my little sister, and my father. Many came and went, and held committees, and examined ledgers and safes, and papers and desks, and drew up forms, and signed signatures, and wound up affairs, never heeding or asking for me till all was over; and I was invited to meet them, and hear that my father was ruined, and everything must be sold to meet the creditors. Very kindly, on the whole, did these men of business deal with me, in spite of their hard looks. I had been quite prepared for all that had come to pass; somehow I had been put unconsciously in knowledge of all these things. One old man, whom I had remembered at my father's table, came forward, and speaking even tenderly and delicately, offered his home to me while the sale went on at least, and for so long a time as I should afterwards need, but I declined. So this last week ended, and brought at its close the last Sunday I should ever spend in the old house. I wondered that Gertrude had not been to see me, had not even written to me; a short note of condolence came from her father, he was away from town, and could not attend the funeral. "I wish she had written me a line," I kept saying; but I resolved that no evil dreams should break this last Sabbath at home. "Let no unfaithfulness be in me to-day," I said,—"the last, the last."

Yet beneath the surface of my tranquillity there ran an undercurrent of turbulent doubtings, so that oftentimes I caught myself longing for the morrow, that I might see Gertrude, and tell her all that I had resolved upon, and release her from our childish engagement. How I loved her, yet the close presence of that other grief nerved me to support this also. At night I was sore troubled with dreams, more than I had ever been before; kept awaking from them, and then sleeping on again, and continuing the vision that had startled me; they changed and glided from one to another form with that mocking semblance of reason that makes them so real; towards morning came one that I remembered afterwards, because of what followed. I had gone down the street in which we lived, and passed immediately into a strange country I had never seen before; for miles away it was overgrown with a forest of funeral plumes instead of trees; suddenly some one was laughing above me, and the laugh, I thought, was Gertrude's, and looking up, I saw her standing on a platform that was near me; and while I yet looked there was another had come beside her, and they were both laughing together, I thought, at me. Whereat I grew angry, and an inexpressibly painful sensation came over me, while quickly, quite imperceptibly, I was struggling in water, and they still above me, leaning over the parapet of a bridge and laughing. I caught a rope that hung from the summit to within a foot above my head, and while my hand closed upon it, it became suddenly, I thought, a pistol, and with a quick, sharp clapping at my ear, shot me through; and the laughter died away upon the parapet far above me. I woke with the pain in my head as if I had been really shot, while my heart beat audibly, and heard a sharp rapping at my door. "It's eight o'clock, sir; you told me to call you at seven, but I couldn't this last morning, sir."

Poor old John, the oldest servant of our house, who had known my father from a child. I bade him enter; I scarcely think he could have slept all night. Then I dressed carefully, break-fasted, and bade all the servants God speed. I would have given them some memorials of my father and of me, but could not honestly, for everything was to be sold, everything, so completely ruined were we. So I spoke to them and talked about their future prospects, and wept as they sobbed again to part with me; for my father was gentle to his servants, and spoke ever kindly to them, and they had remained, all of them, many years in our house.

The last two or three hours were busily spent in gathering to-gether and destroying whatever papers or letters I had, whose use or pleasure had gone, and this had left me little time for thinking; but once in the street, no longer face to face with bitter memories, the perplexities of my future came upon me with the fury of a whirlwind. I had determined to see Gertrude that morning, to release her from her early promise, made when the world was all beyond her and unknown, and in days when I was her hero all unrivalled. I could not blame her, not much at least, that she found many more brilliant than I had ever been; no, I would act as bravely and manfully that morning as became my father's son: yet my resolution nearly choked my life. I tried to think of her father's moneyed pride, and my own ruin, but could not; now that I was going to give up my treasure I felt only how I loved it, yet I had not come without counting the cost. Through the long week that followed my father's burial I had come through bitter tribulation and searing of the heart to what I had determined. Yet as I neared the street in which she lived, the quick pulsation of my heart would catch my breath, and send me staggering along. So clear it seemed to me before, all the words that I should say; but now they all melted away from my hold, and I walked on as one blinded by some fearful sight. Oh! it was much to lose; how much, who shall ever say? who shall make a reckoning of woe like this? but so short time past how smoothly went my life. Six months back I had gone to meet her at the port where she landed, and my future years were then coloured with the colour of the golden sunset that we walked in together on the close of that summer day. And now how was it with me, and with him who had given me life, and her who had made it dear?

I walked through many needless streets, because of the violent beating at my heart; and when it had somewhat ceased, I began to near the house of my doom. I had reached it soon, and was at the door; it opened to let some one pass out. "Is Miss Aymas at home?" "Yes, sir," "I wish to see her alone, you need not give my name, say a gentleman wishes to see her for a few moments." The servant led me into the drawing-room. I entered, and was quite alone. As I crossed the room the reflection of my mourning dress, in a full length mirror, quite startled me; a foolish fright, but my heart stood ready to leap at everything. There was the water-colour I had commissioned a young artist friend of mine to paint for her, hanging in the room. I had never seen it, and now approached it, if by any means it could divert my over-strained expectation. There was drawn the figure of a lonely man standing before a city, iron-walled and turretted, and gar-risoned with a multitude that stood above the gates; but the background of the city was fire, and those thousand or more who kept the gates stood black against the yellow light, and the fire, which was the atmosphere of the city, glowed through the iron grating that barred the going in, and fell upon the dead water of the moat round about, heavily and dull, and upon the pale face of the man who stood there, "at war 'twixt will and will not in his mind;" and I knew it for Dante, and his vision of the city of hell. The picture was wrought wonderfully, as I knew it would be, knowing the artist, and his soul, from boyhood. There was neither play nor forked struggling in that fire, but only glow— the quietness of omnipotent strength. Strange that it held me so—came upon me like a thought, long lost and forgotten, newly found; the visage of the man too, it seemed scarcely definite, else the great heart of the painter beat too stormily when he came to that, and his hand refused obedience; for, assuredly, the face was not at all unlike my own, but older, many years older. I clung fixedly upon the pictured prophecy with the eyes of a drowning man when they fasten piteously upon the white clouds that drift across his face, so near they seem to him looking upwards. My heart had so died within me, that, for a while, I saw as one who sees not, to whom all things are alike unreal; for the room, and all within it, shrunk into unreality, seemed as unreal as the picture, and in the lapsing of my soul into the dream of the picture, the action seemed reversed, and I appeared awakening from a sleep of troubles and dilemmas. A footstep descending to the level of the room convulsed me for a moment—the dream of unreality was gone; the door opened and I was face to face, with Gertrude: she was pale, in her black dress, I thought she trembled slightly as I took her hand. "You have received Papa's note," she asked, "this morning?" I shook my head in answer. She seemed strangely confused, and a painful suspense of silence followed. "Do you stay long in town?" she asked presently. I answered that my plans were unsettled, wondering at the strangeness of the question, and the nervous manner of her speech. Finding I did not even speak now, she went on: "We go to-day to Scotland." I looked up as soon as this was said, and fixed my eyes upon her. "And you were going away without seeing me, cousin, or even writing to me?"

How hotly the fire was burning there behind the walls, in the city of Dis, upon the brows of that solitary man it struck hotly, but upon my brows how cold drops of moisture hung! But I gathered breath and spoke passionately. "Oh, Gertrude, you have been very cruel to me in my bitterness." For a moment a cataract of tears stood ready to fall, and I could not see for them. She laid her hand convulsively upon my arm, and said, "I must stop no more; I cannot bear to see you after all that I have done; we ought not to have met in this way, you will see why, when you read my father's letter; try to forgive me sometime." And when I looked again she was gone.

The seasons came and went continually, as in the former days. I saw the changing of the moon, and the rising and falling of old constellations, as in the beginning of years; and round about the land the ancient winds were blowing and the old sea waves beating, when I left my country, for my great woe had not fallen upon them, nor caused that that dark river should cease to flow for other men as it had ceased for me. There was not anything in all the earth to comprehend my woe.

Away, and across the sea to France, flying from that city of homeless streets weak and sick, and going mad, for I did not mistake the signs that visited me too surely, a startling crushing sense of memory leaving me altogether—and one fixed thought that never left me, but came soothing me at all hours of the day and night—a prophetical foresight of speedy death—onwards, ever onwards, travelling southward, losing memory, growing strange and unknown to my own self. And, as I journeyed on, from day to day, for long weeks, it seemed in some weird trance, all the land before me ripened slowly into corn-fields, flowered into infinite sweet gardens, stretching seaward, stretching sunward, miles away. But, somehow, human faces grew ever vague and indistinct and shadowy, passed close beside me, but yet seemed far off and out of hearing. But I took comfort from the corn-flowers and the deep scarlet poppies; for I lay among them in the quiet morning, all my length among them, waiting, waiting for some fulfilment, I could not remember what, but thought it would surely come at last when they cut away the corn, and the blue and purple flowers, and darkened the sweet skies with rain and wind and cloud, and drove me from them. But, though I travelled ever ceaselessly, I came upon no more flower-lands; but, one night, instead, I came within sight—oh! my poor head—of home again;—saw surely the red fires of London divide the earth and sky, with a long chain of broken lights; knew that the time was come at length—that when I reached the river-side, all would be forgotten, no more cold and hunger, and homelessness for me, no more rain and wind—but a land of corn and cornflowers, and the blue sky above.

By the river bank at length, changed from when I stood there last, but that was long, long ago: there was a moving in the chimes, and they rang out the hour of four, and a quick, immemorial pang shot through me, and I was falling—falling—falling.

The fragrance of freshly-gathered flowers was about me as I

lay softly somewhere when life returned to me; my eyes rested on unfamiliar objects. I was lying on a bed in some strange room; it seemed my waking had been looked for, watched for: I was not alone. Slowly, very slowly, my vision took in the figures of the two who stood beside my bed; a lady, oh! so wonderfully beautiful to look upon, and a man, who might be her father, tall and bronzed and gray with years. My eyes rested upon them both tranquilly, with no painful feeling of strangeness nor sense of curiosity; so filled I was with their beauty, that when the father spoke to me, his words came strange; I could not understand them; and all the while, with wide, deep eyes, the lady looked at me, and there was pity in her stedfast look; then the man spoke again, in a gentle and low voice, and again I felt the pain of uncomprehended speech; he must have seen my perplexity: gradually, very gradually, all that I had suffered came upon me; one by one all the broken links were gathered up, and I remembered my journey, and knew that I was in France, away from my country. Perhaps he saw the gleam of re-born intelligence lighten up my forehead, for he spoke to the lady, and she passed away from the room. He spoke again,—I could hear him now,—kindly and soothingly, felt my hand and my forehead, bathed it till it gathered coolness, and gave me to drink, for my lips were parched; then I slept again, dreamfully, and woke about the time of sunset; the man was no longer in the room, but beside my bed she sat working, and I lay looking at her beauty, regarding her long before she raised her eyes and met my upward gaze. For a moment she was startled, then came near and bent over me: "Hush! you must be quite still; you must not speak yet." She spoke English to me, yet, in spite of her anxious looks and uplifted finger I asked where I was. "In Paris; you have been very ill—near to death; but hush! presently you shall know all: sleep again!" so I looked at her till my eyelids closed, and slept and woke again, ever to find her working steadily close beside me, ever to be gently chidden when I spoke; and the sweet incense of flowers ceased not to hang about the room. Day increased and sunk again, and found her always keeping vigil; and at midnight also she was not wanting, for after quiet days came nights of feverous dreaming, tumultuous, tempestuous, out of

which I started with a loud cry at some unutterable horror and
perplexity, saw the dim light burning in a corner of the room,
and the large shadow of the watcher on the wall, with her head
bowed above me, and, raising lifeless eyes, met ever that one
sweet face, that mingled not with my dreams nor ever sanctified
them. Ah! those dreams of mine—of unutterable woe, of frightful forms and horrible,—faces all inhuman, but with human
meaning,—leering, writhing, swelling, expanding, ever pursuing; of rooted footsteps in high desolate landings, when a tread is
close behind, and a loud ringing noise, like the sound that lives in
shells, comes booming up, increasing and growing louder from
that chamber there, which no man ever enters, because of the
fearful thing that is and is not therein.

But, as days and weeks went on, these also passed away, and I
lay weak indeed, and not far from the limits of life and death, but
my understanding darkened no more. So about the end of summer, I sat upright near the window of the room, and Onore was
with me, for she seldom left her place beside me, and quietly I
drew from her all that had happened, and how it had come to
pass that I was there: then she told me how in the last winter, on
a February morning early, at the end of the month, the 28th—
she should never forget the day—her father was called up (he
was a physician) to see the body of a young man, an Englishman
they said, who had been rescued from the river an hour before,
and lay at the station close at hand, and, as they thought, dead.
And because he pitied me so deeply for my woe-worn face, and
desolation, and because the face was like some one he remembered, and because I was a stranger, and from the land where he
had lived and loved and wedded, he took me to his home, and
nursed and tended me; but I saw, or thought I saw, a paleness in
the beautiful face of my nurse; and I thought, "If I have caused
this, it will be worse than all the evil that has befallen me."

Every day we sat together, and spoke of many things, not any
longer of past sorrow; and she told me of her hitherto life, which
I most longed to hear, and of her father's goodness and his noble
acts; and here she blushed and her sweet voice trembled; never
voice of singing bird, or wind among the trees was more musical
than hers. I thought of her as of the King's daughter in the Song

of songs, "Her lips are like a thread of scarlet, and her speech is comely." She looked most queenly from her dark and regal eyes.

One day towards the end of the year, she took out of her writing-desk some letters of her mother's, and read them to me, for she loved to talk of her mother, and to dwell upon the fact that she was an Englishwoman; from her she had learnt to speak so easily, and as she read on, with her voice ringing clear, events, and names, and dates caused me to bend all my listening to their purport, and forget the voice for a little while; they were all familiar to me, nay, my own name came over and over again, I wondered if I were really sane, and whether my madness had indeed quite passed away. How I was listening now, trembling lest it should not be true, and I be cheated and fooled with accidents; but as she read on I was more confirmed, and laughed with a laugh of triumph, and held her fast, crying, "Onore, it was your cousin that you saved." No more, for a faint feeling passed through me and rapidly left me. Then I told her all my life past for the first time, omitting nothing; and there, in the morning of the New Year, I spoke also of my love for her, deep, intense, enduring; and whether she sorrowed for my sorrows, and pitied me for my griefs, so many and so cruel; or whether she really loved the thing she had saved I know not; but there in the golden winter morning, by the fireside, bright and warm, did she hold my hand in hers, and kiss my forehead, saying, "Dost thou indeed love me as I have loved thee?"

It is a morning in May upon the hill of Canteleu; we are walking, my wife and I, talking lowly from the depth of happiness, upon the brow of the winding road. And below us is the valley and the river, and the city of the towers, and all above the heavens are overlaid with happy blue. A wind is somewhere passing in the upper air, driving the thin white clouds in furious whirls across the sky, and causing it to descend as it were in a quivering rain of blue, but where we stand no wind stirs the grasses. It is our marriage day. I am happy now, quite happy, for a sweet plant is growing in the garden of my soul, and my spirit walks there, desolate no more, nor wounded with its ancient grief. Only sometimes, very rarely for a flash of time, there is a sudden unlocking and unsealing of folded memories, and for a moment I walk again by dark waters, in some lone forest upon windy hills, and hear voices inarticulate like something heard before; smell a savour of flowers as if I had lived the life of flowers in incorporeal existence, and at such times I gather hints and traces of an unrecorded time, for in the reckoning of my life there is a missing year.

A Story of the North

By Edward Burne-Jones

Chapter 1

I walked upon the coast of Denmark that faced the north, all one winter morning, looking at the passing of the ships to and fro upon the deep green sea, as they carried freight of precious merchandise between one land and another; and there was something in the deep purple margin of the sea, and the long white line of breakers, and the flashing of the sunlight upon distant sails, that gleamed for a moment and were gone, and something in the mournful wailing of the old sea-winds as they sung an ancient song among the rocks, that brought up a vision of that sea as it looked many hundred years ago on such a morning to brave and loving eyes that trust and look no more. And I thanked Our Father and blessed Him for the sympathy of sea and wind and cloud that day. "These," said I, "abide for ever, watching the work of human life upon the land: all the earth is changed, and different in every generation, for where the pleas-ant valley was is the tumultuous city, and where the city, is the barren waste; but the sea and clouds looked even thus a thou-sand years ago, and some such music made the sea-winds in the ears of men." On that day, moreover, I was filled with sadness and unquietness of heart, thinking upon the days that are past, and because so much majesty and glory had clean gone out of sight without a record. "Alas!" I said, "for I could weep and weep to think of it, so many noble deeds accomplished, so many deeds of love and holy sacrifice, so many, many gentle hearts broken in far-off times, there in the North, whereof no memory nor record comes to us, no answer from the invisible winds that have seen all and will not speak." Therefore my heart was very heavy for love of all the silent great ones that are not named among men; "yet," I thought, "surely when the day comes at last, after long tarrying, for the great sea to give up its dead, it will happen that the Past also shall render up the keys of its mystery-room, and as it were with stars, whereof Astronomers tell us that their light has not reached the earth, though they shine somewhere gloriously evermore, all the heaven will be a-light with new constellations, brighter, it may be, some of them, than any seen before, than all we have honoured heretofore; new heroes, greater than the old ones, or all as great." With this I comforted my heart: "Shall not the Judge of all the earth do right?" Fitfully there came along the wind a broken carol of the bells in the valley just below. "Ah!" I thought, "for the bitter life of all who lived before Christ and hope were born together, and those bells rang out such happy tunes. What to them seemed Life and Death and Hereafter?" Then I remembered what holy words the poet of my own land—dear country I shall never see again until I dwell there after death—had sung about Yuletime; and I said aloud those hopeful words of his about God's hidden purposes in man, in the hearing of the sea-birds saying,

> "And he, shall he,
> Man, her last work, who seem'd so fair,
>   Such splendid purpose in his eyes,
>   Who roll'd the psalm to wintry skies,
> Who built him fanes of fruitless prayer,
>
> Who trusted God was love indeed,
>   And love Creation's final law,—

Though Nature, red in tooth and claw
With ravine, shriek'd against his creed,—

Who loved, who suffer'd countless ills,
Who battled for the True, the Just,
Be blown about the desert dust,
Or seal'd within the iron hills?"

After this, I sat upon the beach at the foot of a cliff, white as the cliffs of my own country, and took a volume of illuminated writing, and opened at the first page; dark green and purple and melancholy gold lay upon the page and round above the writing; very sad and pensive was the colouring; and in among the flowers and interlacings of delicate branches, long-leaved branches, showed a castle tower grey against a sky of windy blue, and a lady leaned therefrom in the tower-window, resting her white forehead on her right hand, and playing dreamily with her left among the leaves, and an agony of long expectation sealed itself upon her face.

Then so did that pale anguish, that had gnawed upon her bloom of life, hold me tranced, that I read as if in a charmed book, and the mournful colour of the page and the sadness of the lady wrought a vision of the past to this effect.

Chapter 2

I saw it now, clear as in a picture, that castle on the far-off coast of Norway, as it stood up fair and manfully against the breakers of the Northern Sea; and the sea-winds and mountain-winds met above its towers, and contended there, flouting the ancient banners of the kingly house of Elstein. Travellers in that distant land, going through the mountain-pass and valley where the town lay once, walk down to the beach-line, looking at the furious beating of the sea-waves that have not ceased to flow, are blown upon by the same old winds that sang through the pine-forest ages long ago; for those winds, visiting all lands within the upper zone, returning, finding all things changed from when they left the mountain-gorge years before, are still the same. No man now, passing through the valley, thinks ever of the people that dwelt there, happy and brave; thinks ever of their sorrows and their love, nor their broken lives, nor noble deaths.

And this castle faced the sea westwards and northwards, but behind it and to south of it lay a fair valley, sheltered by the rock on which the castle stood from all the north winds, and by the mountains from the east wind; and in the valley below the castle-hill stood the little town, busy and full of traffic; for though hunters on the mountains, who had pierced the dark pine-forest, brought tidings only of the ranges stretching on every side, like a great frozen sea petrified, with all its waves in act of tossing, yet seawards came traders to the town, with news of other lands and the rise of cities in the South; at times also came a message or a gift from one who had left them long before in quest of adventures, and to whom the memory of his birth-land had not ceased to be beautiful, though he should never return. It was pleasant to talk together at the door of the old armourer's in the morning, while the red fire burned merrily in the furnace, and listen to the ringing of the metal plates, as he fashioned armour for heroes, and proved the good sword-blades for battle; for never morning came but some fresh thing had happened to serve for telling. But it was even pleasanter at night-time, hearing fire-light stories, fit for those large shadows on the ceiling and the walls—tales of generations passed long ago. And this was the custom of Hakon the armourer, to have a gathering of the neighbours every night to hear his stories and drink with him. And there at the feet of Gertha his foster-mother, grew the little Engeltram in fear and wonder, listening to those weird legends that fell from Hakon's mouth with such a stately flow, and learning much about heaven and earth and gods and men. And as he grew up to greater understanding, he loved still to hear those legends, and to think that whether true or not, they yet were true in this, that there lies in life, concealed somewhere, more than can be seen by all men; some better and more excellent thing than drinking in the mead-cup and singing loud wassail-songs in festival. Very loving and tender was he in his life, and Hakon and Gertha loved him as their own child, suffered him in all things, hoped and plotted for his welfare, till he grew to manhood. Now Engeltram was pale and hazel-eyed, and his hair fell about his shoulders long and brown and dark; his eyes, moreover, had the seeming of one who ever looks at some fair and far-off object, and cannot yet be satisfied with gazing; for both by day and night there stood before him in his vision the Lady Irminhilda, daughter of King Eric, who lived in Elstein. Through long years they had grown together, as a passion-flower and lily in a desolate wind-swept garden; in the spring-time of their years playing on the hills at the game of king and queen, while the sun passed overhead to warm them, laughed and mocked their little royalty with lengthened shadows on the grass. There he made a crown for her of ashberries and hedge-flowers, and crowned her in the morning of their life; but Vorsimund her kinsman, cruel Vorsimund, he who chased all gentle harmless creatures for his pastime, came between them like a shadow, broke the little crown of ash-tree, and waited ever to torment them with his cruelty and malice. But those years went over, and brought the summer-time of life, warmer suns, and quicker thoughts, and livelier hopes; for Vorsimund had gone for ever and left them, therefore it could not be but long companionship should bring reliance and dependence, and from this a continual want in separation and completeness in communion, till last of all, they seemed divided halves of one same life, that must be joined together lest both should perish. And this was the love that was between them, fast-enduring, and sanctified by many memories, and prepared for suffering and trial in evil days.

But Eric the king, her father, purposed, in his quiet scheming, to add kingdom to kingdom through his daughter, for she was his only child, and to leave behind him a name to be praised and had in honour as the founder of a nation; and this was the sin of Eric, that he had respect to long futurity and what might be said of him in days to come, and counted not the present time as anything, nor the happiness of living men to be compared with this poor fame of his; wherefore all wise men would judge that evil was already threatening, and would not fail to overtake him presently.

Chapter 3

There was high festival in the castle of Elstein, among lords
and elders and strangers, who had come from distant lands to be
guests with Eric while the feasting lasted. Now he had pro-
claimed this festivity in honour of his daughter upon her twen-
tieth birthday; and he looked that some fortunate issue to his
proud hopes would follow, and that the fame of her great beauty
might be spread abroad wherever the strangers travelled. All his
scheming and ambition was known to the lovers, for Engeltram
had found but little favour or forbearance from him lately, and
judged that this was the reason; but herein he thought wrongly,
for Eric, because he was over-reaching, was short-sighted also,
and suspected nothing of all that passed so near him; but he
hated Engeltram for his strange resemblance to one you shall
hear of presently, who had destroyed his plans in other days, and
whom he had hated with a very deadly hatred. So upon this
night of the festival, before all the lords and chiefs among the
people, King Eric made a royal oath, that no man who was not
kingly born and dowered with wide dominions, should wed the
Lady Irminhilda. And Engeltram when he heard the words, left
the banquet straightway, burning with indignation, for he
thought they had respect to him chiefly, and that the eyes of all
who knew him were set stedfastly upon him.

Now within the castle that stood four-sided, facing the four
chief winds, was a court-yard, and upon the eastern side a
covered balcony of woodwork looking into it and open towards
it. Many a time had royal children played there in wild weather,
and kings walked there looking how it fared at sea, for the balcony was high above the ground, and overlooked the west walls
to the sea beyond. There leaned Engeltram when the moon was
high. The Lady Irminhilda passed him going to her chamber
from the banquet, for the revel and the drinking had begun:
pale was she and faltered in her footsteps, only the sight of him
forlorn and leaning there, sent the life blood to her cheeks again.
He saw her come and stand beside him; looking unchanged, unutterable love from deep blue eyes. "I knew that you would
come," he said; "at that moment I was bending all my soul to this

one desire that you would come, and it prevailed to draw you here; nevermore shall I have doubt that we are one together for life and death." She looked upwards gently, wonderingly, sad to think how grief had made his musical sweet voice so hoarse and hollow, yet she spoke no word. "Oh! I have seen it, seen it clearly in deep sleep, the beautiful garden westwards and the fourfold river through it, and the tree with crimson fruit; and last night I dreamt of it again, and saw moreover her whom I never saw before, my mother, standing in deep grass and calling; at first I thought that it was you, but it could not be, for you were beside me, looking also. Ah! she was so strangely like you." In the recollection of his dream he stopped awhile to linger; she spoke no word nor interrupted, only looked stedfastly and sadly. "It will be a dark and fearful night, and no man will leave the fireside nor the festival till morning; come, and I will carry you to the home that I have seen in dreams." She saw the moonlight for a moment lying on the water, making a great highway to the west, then a flash of regal disdain lighted up her quiet eyes, but died again at sight of those worn cheeks and sound of that hoarse voice. "I may not so leave my father's house," she answered coldly; "the night is dark, but treacherous heart knows greater darkness; I may not leave him so: could you rob the old man at such an hour, when he cannot follow nor pursue? it would be a brave thing truly." He fretted at the swordless baldric that was slung about him, coldness had no charm to quiet him, and her words fell with a dull and muffled sound upon his ears. She was so grieved that she had spoken so, when the words were past recalling; what was all her queenly right, and a line of ancient kings at such an hour, in such a presence! She would have died with him there, gladly. "Oh! Engeltram, be Engeltram once more before I leave you! Such a one I knew, gentle and good, wearing truest armour of nobility, and I thought him a hidden king, but just now he passed out somewhere, and I shall go and look for him;" poor heart! making merry in its breaking.

At her feet he fell down straightway, kneeling, sobbing out his spirit to her, holding by her folded dress as the dying hold by life. In that hour she was the stronger of the twain. "Hush," she said; "not so, not so, for now art thou indeed my Engeltram once more." In the pauses of the sobbing of his breath you might hear her weeping gently, raining down a summer shower of tears upon his drouth of life; then she raised him, kissed him gaily, bade him lovingly remember all his former gentleness, and use it for her sake. "I shall wait for you, my hero, till you come." It was pitiful to see him stretch out arms of vain beseeching, arms that should never clasp her more: twice she turned and looked upon him, at feud in her divided will, for the outstretching of those dear arms seemed still to draw her in the face of will; but when the door closed with a rough and jarring sound upon his ears then he rose up, cried "Irminhilda" once, with such passionate yearning, and prolongation of the name, that all his soul seemed spent in it. Ever after, in the solemn midnight a voice went crying with a bitter cry of supplication through all the chambers of her soul, winding with the mournful echo of cavernous depths, "Irminhilda."

Chapter 4

At midnight he passed out into the thick darkness: from every quarter under heaven did the armies of the winds gather together for battle; the noise of the mustering of their legions came from the outer sea with a long, low, sullen rumbling, like the sound of a multitude of chariots in mountainous lands: it was a night of storm and wind to be remembered even on that fearful coast. The great sea had gone down a little space, and left a narrow band of shore behind it; there he walked till the sea came up again, and his great heart was broken within him, and all his inner life dark and full of tempest like the night. "Ah! when will it be over? all my strength is departed from me, I am grown untimely like a leaf in winter." By the rock of plighted vows he watched the mighty sea, drawn up by unknown influences, flood all the space where he had walked an hour before; somewhere a contest of strength raged among the winds, for they rose and shrieked through the air, fell again and buffeted the waves about, lashing up the white foam, and driving it in sheets across the land. All the dwellers in the town hard by, and the revellers in the castle, and all who lived upon the coast, trembled that night and could not sleep; from the sea and from the forest came strange wailings, cries of men mingled with the sobbing of the waters. In the old armourer's room sat a company who had met for merriment; none dared so much as leave the threshold, for they were feeble with the weight of years, but sat there all night long, and muttered lowly by the fireside, telling sometimes stories of other storms and greater, long ago.

In that hour came Death and strove with Engeltram. He beheld him like a fair young hero standing by the water edge; all his face was calm and tranquil, and his armour gleamed upon him whenever the moon looked out through riven spaces in the darkness. No sword nor shield had he, nor any weapon of encounter, and to Engeltram it seemed his helmet blossomed with white star flowers, set about with leaves; but withal there was no hope nor beauty in his eyes to rest on, nor colour of life upon his cheeks, so that looking at him you might not call him either fair or faulty.

"Who art thou, so peaceful and silent, and why hast thou come to me?"

"They that dread me call me Death, but from them my name is secret. I bring rest to weary people, and forgetfulness of sorrow."

"Thy face is very still and quiet, fixed and dreamy; to-day I saw my own face, it was marred with cruel furrows and its former beauty gone: almost I seem to love thee even now, with the love of some remembrance, I know not what."

"Yes, for I came to thee once before, and shall come again, and at that time you shall know me and call me rightly; until then my name is hidden."

All night long they strove together, wrestled by the margin of the sea, by the rock of plighted vows; all the winds rushed out together from the sea-caves and mountain passes, and fought above them till the morning. Once the moon came out full-orbed and lonely, and looked upon them; and for a moment one great shadow of the mortal hero, lay vast and huge along the ground. "Ah!" thought he, "it will be so then, and I shall lie there presently;" and ever his arms grew fainter, and his knees beneath him shook and trembled, but the grasp of the other never slackened. So they swayed upon the rock to and fro. One looking afar off, and knowing not the fierce encounter, nor the cause, would have thought it a tall and stately tree bending to the fury of the winds, so closely knit together were they. And when in the close locking of their arms together, Engeltram looked into the other's face, he beheld it calm and peaceful as before, and a dreamy look in those lorn eyes that hinted of some great unexerted strength. "Oh! thou bright being, I shall fail before thee presently." Yet the purple twilight of the morning came, passed overhead and by them, and with it went the winds to blow about the islands of the outer seas, and far-off countries; still they wrestled on together. And about the hour of morning Engeltram felt that his limbs grew stronger, and the sinews of his great frame stood like cords about his arms, and gathered force; but the power of the other weakened fast, and his grasp grew fainter and fainter: and when next Engeltram looked into his face about the time of sunrise, he wondered greatly, for there was no longer any beauty in him, but ghastly pallor, and in place of that tranquillity had come a slumbrous, dreamy void, expressionless. But when the sun was fully up, and the sweet morning light lay upon the outer edge of castle, hill and tree, and the long, long wings of cloud, rosy-red, that came up with the sun, stretched out further to the north and south, as they would zone all the base of the great firmament with a girdle of crimson and gold, then Engeltram found himself alone, weak but living.

All about him sprang great beauty, everything lay robed in light, lay coloured with the tints of morning, and the summer birds sang overhead a merry song of victory; there was no sign of battle anywhere, in sea or sky or land; they had passed away with the passing of that fearful night; and with the morning came this calm.

Chapter 5

Then he arose and went homewards; somehow there was transfiguration in his face and strange radiance upon his forehead as he stepped into the armourer's forge; he looked so like a man who has seen a vision and will not live for long. All that summer's day he laboured at the forge, fashioning for himself a sword; not a moment did he give for resting or looking upwards, though never morning was apparelled in raiment of sweeter colours than was this, that followed on the storm. At the hour when shadows lengthen, he saw the spaces of light upon the floor that came through the doorway and the window darken with the passers by; sometimes they would stay and watch him, yet he never gave them greeting nor looked up. It was as if his pent-up wrath found outward satisfaction in so raising a thunderstorm of iron hailstones on the anvil, and listening to the answer of salute from helmet, shield and spear, as they shook and rattled against the wall. From another part of the armoury old Hakon worked and watched him, never spoke nor asked him question, for it was his custom to be silent in perplexity, nor "dignify an impaired thought with breath"; for he knew well some grievous calamity had fallen on the young man. By nighttime he had finished his labour, stood before his foster-father with the sword of his working in his hands; long and wide showed the blade in the gleaming of the furnace-light. "Ah!" laughed Engeltram in triumph, for the fire ran adown the blade like blood; "my father's sword lies rusting in his grave upon the barren hill, he left me neither sword nor name to keep; so you see, dear Hakon, I must make them for myself." There was neither wonder nor curiosity in the face of the old man, he seemed to be always looking for some unheard-of deed to spring from the lad; he only answered such words of comfort as came to him. "It is a better thing, my son, to leave behind us a good name, than to receive it." But Gertha asked, "What has happened to thee, my child? come and tell me all, and why thy life is so overcast." And the youth laid his head upon her lap, as he used to do in other days, when he was a child and was weary of play, and told her all his sorrow, while the sunset lingered yet upon the earth, saying, "Thus and thus did the king speak before his lords and men, and swore an oath before them, but as for me I have greatly desired to die and be at rest."

"Listen to a tale, my child, for it seems thou art again my child lying so, and many strange and unheard-of stories I used to tell thee thus." Something in his childlike purity, and simple confidence brought back a vivid memory to her, he looked so like the little Engeltram of twenty years ago. Through a wall of partition, they could hear from time to time the deep voice of Hakon and his companions, talking of the last night's storm, and one that they remembered on the night when the old king died. Then Gertha spoke: "It was in the lifetime of King Asmundur that I served the Lady Hilda, his only daughter, and was first among the maidens that waited on her. She was so like her brother's daughter, whom thou lovest, that I need not say how fair she was, and wonderfully formed; all the people loved her, I too, more than anything in life, though she was ever wayward, and spoke not always gently, but had bitter words and cold ones, even for those she loved."

"Then," said Engeltram, looking up, "she was not like the Lady Irminhilda, and her great beauty did belie her acts; to be ungentle in her beauty would destroy it." "Nay, but she was beautiful, and I loved her for her pride, and would not have it otherwise; but the strangest thing to see was the love that the grim old king her father, bore to her, and in strangewise did it show itself: none, I think, who trembled at the presence of the rough-speaking king, knew aught of that fierce love for his daughter. His son walked moodily through the halls, and his father seldom spoke to him; for in his countenance shone no light of enterprise, and between them there was little sympathy. I think the old warrior scorned his son, for his own youth-time had been bloody and stormy, and little rest from battle and encounter had he known through life; so, what of good lay in his son was all unfathomed, and pride and sullenness came uppermost. But the Lady Hilda grew up like a plant that flowers late, when all about is winter; like a rose set beside a stormy sunflower. Now, she loved most of all to watch from the window that looks upon the sea, and to sit there, leaning all the summer afternoons, and never speaking; sometimes, my child, I think she must have seen him, who came afterwards, through all the interspace of earth and sea, sitting in his olive garden in the south, and so ardently breathed out her spirit through fixed gazing, that she drew him to her. For, one evening, there came in sight a gallant ship, and it neared the castle one whole hour, while my lady did not cease to draw it with her stedfast-looking, and then it anchored just below the hill where thy father lies. From it stepped one of such lordly growth and bearing, as I had set eyes upon never before, either among my own countrymen or strangers, and so, I fancy, thought my lady from her window. Those that came with him called him Angelus, and the place of his birth that same fair Southern land of which the poets come and sing to us—a summer land they called it, of flowers, and lakes that never freeze. He was tall, like the tallest of our men, but his countenance was altogether different, long and thin and pale, and over his forehead, and low upon his shoulders, fell his long dark hair. I forget how long a time the stranger lived in the castle; it was somewhere in the summer when he came, and he went with the last leaves that fall in autumn. Ah! many summers have come and gone since then, but none so warm and bright as that, when the handsome strangers were guests among the townsmen, like their lord in the castle. I remember that the King, Asmundur, was sorely puzzled by his noble guest, as indeed we all were. Sometimes, after his uncertain manner, he would be rough and uncourteous, and speak defiantly, but always there proceeded from the other such pliancy and gracious habit of forbearance, that forthwith all his wrath and changefulness would melt before him. I think he liked his guest and feared him also; liked him for a power of great persuasiveness that he had not in himself, but wished him gone that he might be the rough and stormy king of old. But Eric hated him, and would not remain in his presence, but spent his time from the castle, plotting evil. I am not wise, my child, but I could see how it fared with my lady's heart before her father's visitor; he bent her to all purposes of his will, her so wayward. Before the darkness of his eye she bent all her nature to obedience. He would ring out music from his harp, singing to it, till she poured out all her life before him. I could not understand him, nor his gracious words, he was so altogether unlike any of the men that I had seen.—Art thou still listening, my child, or has deep sleep overtaken thee?"

"No sleep will come to me, dear Gertha, therefore speak on, and quickly; for I am like a lonely man nearing a height, knowing not whether a great sea, or a barren moor, or a pleasant garden is beyond; but knowing surely that a turning point of life is come." She laid her hands again upon his head, as he bent down, and spoke on, smoothing all the while his hair, and playing with it.

"It was Eric, the king's son, who overheard them, by the rock at the end of the slip of sand, for there they plighted word for ever, and he went in straightway before Asmundur, and told an evil and cruel tale, till the old king stood up so full of wrath and vengeance that none could stand before him. Now, I was in the passage that overlooks the court-yard, and heard all the words that had been spoken, and immediately I ran to the rock where they still stood together, looking more beautiful than ever in the autumn sun, and as I had power, told them, hurriedly and tremblingly, all that had happened; of Eric's betrayal, and the wrath of the king; how he vowed, in my hearing, a cruel death for Angelus; and withal, I was so overtaken with fear, that I caught Angelus by the arm, and pointed to his ship, and therewith he blew his horn three times, long and loud, and his followers gathered swiftly round him; but Hilda lay upon the ground like one dead. He bore her tenderly to the ship, and laid her there insensible of anything. It was all done so rapidly; save only the noise of the horn along the coast there was no signal of departure; and, while Asmundur meditated wrath, and Eric waited for triumph, the gay ship, and all its crew, went sailing with a strong north wind behind them, towards the olive gardens of the south. I know not what passed afterwards in the castle, for I never returned to it, though no one knew what part I had taken in the flight; but I came to the house of Hakon, having been long betrothed to him. Ah! he was strong and warlike then. So I have been happy ever since."—She paused a little time; it was as if the name of Hakon had brought back the memory of very happy days, for a blissful and placid smile came and rested upon her countenance. His voice came in these pauses of her story, through the walls of the room where he sat, talking with the neighbours, telling, it may be, even then, of his own first love for Gertha, and the deed for which she loved him, in that black forest that lay eastward; his voice, how changed from that time, when it went ringing down the pass with the war-cry of Asmundur.

Engeltram looked up into her gentle face; time had wrought kindly there, in the treading of its footsteps had blanched the roses of her cheeks to lilies only; but when again she spoke he sunk his head as before.

"A happy time. For I could not but think my fair mistress would be happy with such a loving husband, across the sea; yet, there would come seasons of sorrow doubtless to her, whenever the north wind blew, and the swallows came southwards, telling of a dreary winter in the north, for that old desolate king, who loved her well. He never came from the room where he stood when the tidings of her flight reached him; we never heard the ringing of his sword and spear, nor his old war-cry again. But, one winter's night, six years afterwards, there blew a great hurricane at sea, all night long; so wild and furious as I remember not any before or after, till last night. We had been keeping Yule festival. Old men of our town had never witnessed anything so fearful. From time to time came cries of dying people from the sea, of drowning men from sinking ships, and every wind wailed like a troubled spirit along the coast. Hakon sat here with me alone, we had not spoken since the storm began. About an hour before midnight, there went up a loud and bitter cry from the castle, so long and piercing that it seemed no one human voice could have uplifted it; for it rent the thick walls of the castle with its loudness, and was heard above all the violence of the tempest. And when it had quite ceased, Hakon left me, and went running up the hill, and I was left alone. Then it seemed as if the storm, that raved down the street with drenching waters, had driven him back; for the door re-opened, and closed, as I thought, after him. My eyes were fast locked together within my hands, and I sat rocking with terror at the storm; but, when I looked up, wondering he did not speak, I was very frightened; for there stood before me, not Hakon, but Angelus, pale, like a ghost, and drenched with rain, and in his arms a little child. I knew him in a moment, though he looked older; oh! so much older and more sorrowful; all his long dark hair lay matted on his forehead with sea-water, and his clothes hung heavily with wet. I was less frightened then, my child, when I saw thee lying in his arms, sleeping from very weariness, for I knew it could be no spirit."

Engeltram gave no sign of listening by word or upward look, only she felt him tremble violently, and shake through all his limbs.

"He spoke with that deep voice of his, the same as of old, so gentle and sweet. 'I am dying, Gertha; the horrors of this wild night have broken my strength, and all my companions are perished in the storm.' 'And the Lady Hilda,' I cried, impetuously, the rush of blood at my heart choking further utterance. 'She is in my home in the happy south, waiting for me. I came to buy forgiveness of Asmundur with this child, but I die before my promise is fulfilled to her. Take him, dear Gertha, for love of your lady, when I am dead, and tell the king, her father, that Engeltram is my surety, that I will repay him all beyond the grave.' Then, my child, he died, saying, 'Engeltram,' once again, for very love of thy sweet name, and that I might well remember it. The firelight rested on his pale face, till I almost thought he lived again in its glow, and made great shadows of us twain upon the walls, like watching ghosts. All night long I kept a weary watch, singing magic runes above the body of the dead, that his spirit might have rest in its journey to the gods. Thou wast then too young to understand thy woe.

"When the morning came, it was as fair as this, freshening up the valley: so calm and fair a day, as if all cloud and stormy weather had spent itself in the night. I took thee to the window, and opened it, and looked towards the castle with thee lying in my arms, all unconscious of the covered form that lay where it had fallen. Then Hakon passed the window, looking worn and sleepless; and, at the entrance, I told him of the night's adventure, set thee down upon the ground, and took him to thy father's side. Oh! so well I can remember, that thou camest and didst look up between us with wide eyes, and then down upon that which lay covered on the ground; and then didst lay thyself down by the face of him who loved thee, and slept there in that gentle morning. And Hakon told me how the old Asmundur dreamed a fearful dream, and woke up suddenly with a loud cry, and fell straightway on the floor, dead, about an hour before midnight. And because Eric was now king, and because of his hatred to Angelus, we agreed together never to reveal the message, nor deliver thee to danger. I took thee, sleeping in my arms, and nursed thee all that day. Thou wast so weary, little head, all the while that Hakon and his men worked upon the hill-side, and buried Angelus. But thou didst smile and smile, in quiet sleep, all the time through, Engeltram." "Engeltram," she cried presently, for his silence scared her, she could not understand it. He looked up: one seeing his stedfast face had never thought that all this story was new to him, or in anywise affected him. He rose and kissed her, holding her in his arms awhile. The calmness of his look and manner was more terrible to her than all.

Gertha did not sleep that night. It was about morning twilight, that, as she lay by the side of Hakon, there passed before the window, a tall and silent shadow. Hakon was then awake, and he cried out to it, asking who or what it was. And the voice of Engeltram answered, "Come, dear Hakon, and bind on my sword, for, before the sun is up, I must be far upon the sea." Then he went to the side of Gertha, and, stooping down, kissed her lovingly. "Is it so?" she asked. "And now I know that it is well, though I shall never see thee more. She will know thee by the baldric of thy sword, which she wrought for Angelus in my sight; but I shall never see thee more, my son, my son." The voice of Hakon called him from below. "Come and let me gird thy sword on, dear Engeltram, for now I know that one day thou wilt come again and reign over us, cheering my old heart, and Gertha's, with the sight of thee."

Chapter 6

In the third month of his voyaging, while he made still southwards, Engeltram was driven, by contrary winds, to a wild and barren coast. It was about the coming on of winter; so his men besought him that they might harbour there; for the coast everywhere showed roughly; and onwards, as far as they might see, the waters seemed scarcely navigable, among reefs of sharp-pointed slanting cliffs, that shelved off into the sea, suddenly, and appeared again in innumerable islands, marking the place of ancient headlands, that the waves had broken through.

There, upon the shore of a certain bay, they disembarked, and made fast their vessel; and, presently, the near forest rung to the sound of hatchet and pike for the building of winter huts. And Engeltram also worked with them, till all the timber for their houses was felled, making good cheer, and singing, either songs of old heroes, or of seasons and the summer of the pleasant south; but none knew how dark all summer and flower-seasons had grown to him, how one night had changed to darkness all the colour of the skies and hills for him. So, when the wooden huts were now set up along the shore, and his men had begun already to keep Yule festival, with feats of strength and swiftness, Engeltram said to them, "Last night, in the dreaming of my sleep, I saw, upon the rim of land there, where the sky stoops down to meet it, Loki, the great mischiefmaker, with his evil sword of scandal, beckoning, and saying, 'Come, and let us try our strength together;' therefore, I am going, knowing well that some temptation waits for me. Let no man follow nor come with me, but wait here until the spring comes back again, and I return." So, Engeltram left them sorrowful; but no man stirred from his place to follow him; somehow, the voice that called obedience a better thing than sacrifice had taught them this.

But Engeltram saw no more of Loki, neither in dreams nor waking, though he passed a five-days' journey towards the place where he had beheld the armed figure of the god on the horizon's edge; but, on the morning of the sixth day, he came suddenly upon a mighty inland water, dark and deep where overhanging rocks kept out the sun by day, and made long ghostly shadows in the moonlight. It was land-locked everywhere; there was no outlet to the sea on any side; and through a passage between these rocks he came suddenly upon this water. And immediately he heard a sobbing and broken voice near him; and, looking, beheld an old man sitting at the water's edge, weeping bitterly. He went up, therefore, and spoke comfortingly, asking what grief had overtaken him, who looked so old and majestical. And the old man, as it were, from custom of looking to the face of one who speaks, turned where the voice came, and Engeltram saw that he was sightless. "Oh! sir, if you can give me any help, for I am not far from death." And Engeltram said, "What help?"

and the other answered, "I have lived a king among men, over all this country; but blindness overtook me, and I could not lead my armies any more to battle; so, all men forsook me, all but my daughter and my three sons; and her whom I loved more than all my kingdom and my other children, did an enemy come and carry away; and my sons went out, one by one, to fight with that cruel robber, who had come across the sea to trouble me: one by one, and three in number, but they came not back again. I only heard the noise of their conflict in the morning; and, at night, I groped about, and found their bodies each several time, and buried them; but ever since I live here desolate, knowing that Freyda is not far from me, and sometimes sees me, though she can never give me help; for he that stole her from me keeps her in strong durance in the tower at the lake's end." Now, when Engeltram heard this, he was full of indignation, and rattled his sword and shield together, and made a righteous vow upon them that he would bring the king his daughter back again that day, "for I shall win the victory," said he; "the All-Father will not suffer such a thing to be for ever." Then the old king blessed him, and dismissed him, and set himself to listen with all his might. And the hero walked along the water-side a full mile, thinking deeply, and once a faint momentary gleam, unlike a memory, like he knew not what—some indefinable resemblance to something heard before, to something done or suffered in immemorial time—a quick and subtle flash that all was not new, that something most like it had happened long ago, passed through his mind in vague perplexity. And while he still revolved what this might mean, he came to the foot of a tower, that stood half in the water, and opened by the land side; and, as he beat at the doorway with the hilt of his sword, there looked out upon him the beautiful face of one that he knew; for, at first, he thought her Irminhilda, and a painful doubt if all was not a dream, seized him for a moment; but when she spoke he knew not the voice, and took strength to look again. "Art thou the Lady Freyda, daughter of the blind king, that sits for ever by the lake?" and she answered, "I am," with a voice, from which all hope had long departed; and, therewithal, they heard the feet of one coming down the winding steps that led up the rock, and, in a moment after Engeltram was standing face to face with an armed warrior; and it was Vorsimund.

Narrow was the space and laid about with flint stones, but they fought together without word or dally, hand to hand, and foot to foot. No human eye looked upon them—not Freyda's; she could not see him fall, as she had seen her brothers before, and live. When the old king caught the clamour of the conflict, and heard how it was prolonged, and that the stranger had not yet fallen, he rejoiced and sang an old song that had cheered him many a time in battle; and it was answered by Freyda in the tower, and these two kept singing, answering one another with such music as they could, while the air trembled all the rocks with the clashing and the banging of iron arms. And the singing of their voices made a charm over the issue of the battle, for to Engeltram it was sweet music, but to Vorsimund such discord that every blow fell from him, ill-timed and out of measurement, till he grew faint and sick, all the landscape reeling and swimming in his vision. So about the setting of the sun, he fell down upon the sharp flint-stones, and his eyes closed, and his breath left him. Then Engeltram went into the tower, and told Freyda how Vorsimund lay dead upon the earth, and told her also to prepare a place for her father's coming; so he went and brought the blind king, whose heart trembled and beat like the heart of a little child; darkness covered all the earth when they reached the tower, and Engeltram could scarcely see the form of Vorsimund lying dead. That night they told the story of their lives, one to another, the blind king and Engeltram; but Freyda watched the stranger only, waited on him and was silent. "Tomorrow," said Engeltram, "I will go and bury this evil man, for he was my kinsman." But in the morning when he went out to see the body and to bury it, it was not anywhere; and though he sought in every place for many days, late and early, yet no signs were manifest. "Some ravenous beast," he thought, "has carried him off, and devoured him." Yet neither was his armour visible anywhere. Three months he abode with them: in the morning hunting for them, and bringing home such things as he had caught; and in the evening talking with them, and listening as they sang together. But he saw that Freyda ever waited on his words, and hung upon them, and showed in all her silence and her speeches that she loved him very deeply; and because he was good, and pure, and noble, he felt more anguish at this than at all the evils that had yet befallen him, and trembled when he thought how it would end. Yet he could not hinder her, yet he would not be cold to her, that so she might learn the truth; but he suffered all her loving ways which were more sharp than arrows to him, for he saw her daily growing happy, and singing gaily. If ever hope for death possessed him, it was then, chief of all. The blind king saw not anything of all this, but made excuse for her. "It is suffering that has made her silent, when the spring comes she will give you better cheer of words." And when he heard her singing every day more gaily; "Hark! it will be as I have said, when the spring comes round she will be happy." At such times Engeltram could not answer, for he was choked with tears.

"Happier in springtime!" Yes, verily, poor child! much happier than he had looked to; for Engeltram had spoken, and she lay dead, and her father with her, buried by those arms she died in. The grass was growing with fresh blades of resurrection when he went forth, alone, alone, by the way that he had come, and returned again to his ship.

Favourable winds blew on them as they sailed out of the little bay, and went once more into the deep sea. Something in the knowledge that he had not failed in bitter trial, something in the happy brightness of the skies, that never ceased to change and alter, bringing every day new sights to please him; something in his heart that bade him hope in front of sorrow that all might yet be well—after long endurance, after many years, after death, might yet be well—brought him some tranquillity. Whensoever he descended on the coast, he did no harm to the peaceful; neither feeders of flocks upon the hills, nor fishers on the coast; only on the lawless and such as lived by violence, and built for themselves strongholds among the mountains, did he wage continual warfare, late and early rising up and vanquishing; so that in all wild ballads of that land, which is called Ireland, would you hear him praised and honoured; called Avenger and Defender—the beautiful hero that came from Lochlin. His fame moreover spread upon the sea. Who spoke of it? Who carried it?

None could tell; only, as such things are wont to happen, it was known; and he was called great and noble in the ears of Irminhilda; and the eyes of Hakon burned with the fire of other days at mention of his deeds.

Chapter 7

Lamentation in a convent of Madonna on the shore of Sicily; nightly vigil and the voice of weeping from every nun. She whom they called Mother lay near to death, wearily tossing. Pray for her everywhere, all good Christians! she so pure and gentle, holy, and true, lies dying, stricken with fever, and tranced; pray that the passage of her soul be not hindered, but quiet and swift.

Ten long nights, and weary days between them, and the convent has not rested. There is grave perplexity in the faces of the watchers, for words of cherished memory have fallen from her lips, unfathomable to all hearers. Why so stormy a transit for the gentle soul that walked so quietly among her fellows? None may tell. "Watch and pray," said the priest, "we know not the power of the Evil One, but we know the power of God."

On the tenth night, a little before midnight, the fever departed, and she said, "Who called me since I was laid in trance?" but none answered, thinking that the fever had bereft her. "Nay, but one called 'Hilda' quickly, in some need;" and seeing they all wondered still and denied, (for her name among them was Angela,) she sighed, and said softly, "Then he will come presently." It was at the time of darkness, when the good ship that bore Engeltram and his men struck upon the rocks below the convent; for, while the Abbess lay dying, none had hung out lights for mariners. And the ship that had gone through many storms, and borne them bravely until now, went down swiftly into the dark waters, unlighted of moon or star or beacon. And Engeltram raised his voice mightily, and rent a passage through the winds for that cry, "Hilda," and then went deep in the eddy of the waters, that boiled furiously on the ship as it went down.

In the space of a minute after he rose again, and struck out manfully to the shore, calling a second time upon the same name, knowing not how near his course was to fulfilment: at the second cry, Angela lifted herself up, and the radiance of new life was upon her forehead. "Bring him in to me," she said, "and quickly, before I die."

They were together, the mother and the son: at the last hour, after longing and fruitless watching, after many years; so was the good Lord kind to her. Twenty years! and in this brief moment it was overspanned, and made as though it had not been. Spring and autumn, summer and winter, told twenty times! and now it was over, and they had met. For a little space death withdrew himself, while they held converse together, speaking of Angelus; afterwards she told not anything about herself, which he desired chiefly, but spoke only of Christ and resurrection, saying, "We shall be together, Engeltram, even yet." And she kissed him and blessed him there, telling him the meaning of his name, and why it was given him, and how he must teach his people. She said moreover, "Hasten back again to your own place, dear son, and prepare for the receiving of those I send you, and give them fellowship and brotherhood." Again and yet a third time she blessed him, calling him good and dear, and her soul passed about the time of matins, when she and Engeltram were alone.

After many days, wherein he could not speak, nor close his eyes, through his bewilderment, not believing yet that she had gone from him, he remembered her command, that he should go and make ready for those that she would send; and he took ship with all that had escaped the wreck, and steered northwards about midsummer. Overhead went long companies of wild swans, seeking the brief summer in the north, with flutterings of many wings. At evening and at morning he sat apart, in the prow, to think of all that had happened, of his mother Hilda, so late found and early lost, of her precious bequeathal of Belief that he would teach his people: Irminhilda should hear it also and receive it; then he bent his head down low, as if in deep humility or loyal fealty. Hakon also and Gertha would be surely foremost among all that loved and came out to meet him, for he had been gone a year, and had won victory and honour, and done virtuously, and now he was returning home.

Chapter 8

Watching still and waiting, resting her white forehead on her right hand, playing dreamily with her left among the leaves, and an agony of long expectation sealed upon her face—

"She will surely die," they said, all the maids that waited on her.

All night the roar of battle came to them, swelled up the valley to the castle walls, and faded: a noise of baying hounds and screaming curlews mingled with the sullen roar of conflict; a rueful time for timid maids that bore her company. For Engeltram waged a deadly battle among the mountains with an ancient foe, even Vorsimund, whom he had not slain outright by the Irish lake: but this time they were not alone; a thousand or more followed them to battle. Now it had happened thus: when Engeltram came in sight upon the last evening, one ran down the coast who had looked for his arrival night and day, and made signs that he should land there secretly; and the signal was seen from the ship, and there they landed. But Engeltram could not speak for terror, fearing that some evil had befallen Irminhilda; the other, therefore, told him how, three days back, Vorsimund descended suddenly upon the coast, with a band of armed men in ten ships demanding the surrender of the castle and the king's daughter in marriage; and hereupon a fearful battle had followed, wherein Eric had fallen, and Hakon also, leaving the castle with a few defenders, ready to open. "Where is Gertha?" said Engeltram; the other shook his head, answering that she had died quietly in her sleep on the day that Engeltram had left. Then Engeltram gathered together all the men that were armed and scattered over the mountains, and came suddenly upon the host of Vorsimund: so the battle had continued since the time of sunset, and it was now about four in the morning. "What time of the night is it?" said one: another maiden answered, "It wants an hour till morning:" whereat the clamour of the shock of arms ceased suddenly, and a silence followed for a little space, and then a shout, like a shout of triumph, so loud and piercing that it was as if the armies of the winds had lent their voices to that cry; then again a silence deeper than before.

"Listen!" said Irminhilda, and lowered her head to the speech of inaudible voices; "quick, for he has called me twice." Instinctively they brought her fairest robes, and arrayed her in them; broidery of costly workmanship, wrought about with flowers. In her bridal dress she sat upright, looking at the sea no more, listening only; all her senses closed save one; there came only the roar of the tide, and sharp clapping of the breakers down the coast.

Now, Engeltram was dying of his grievous wounds, and his life was ebbing fast to consummation; all around him stood the lords and captains, and the chiefest of the people, speaking none, but weeping only; and so sweet a smile and painless lay upon his features, and so deep tranquillity about his lips and inward triumph in his eyes, that great awe descended on them, made them silent in their grief. It was about the time of morning twilight when Engeltram was dying, and the night was going down behind the sea, swiftly, swiftly, all the stars and clouds together behind the sea.

"The morning is coming," said the lords, "and a fresh wind with it; in an hour the sun will be upon the hilltops;" but Engeltram looked ever westward, though a gathering dimness darkened all his vision into night; it seemed he listened fixedly, hearkening for a signal: presently, with a mighty effort, that drove the blood swiftly through the cruel passage of the sword, he raised himself to listen.—"Hark," he said, "I hear a noise of rowing, and dipping of the oars in water." "It is the lapping of the waves along the beach," said the lords.

Like one fathoms deep in sleep, yet with eyelids open, sat Irminhilda, swaying gently to the converse of invisible presences, as one moves to the tune of instruments, to the measure of musical rhymes. "It is nearly morning," said her maidens, "all the hills are standing ready for the dawn; in an hour the sun will come." But she heard them not, or hearing, seemed to hear not, but continually her head inclined forwards, and her face drooped lower. Neither the warriors at the mountain pass, nor the weary maidens in the chamber heard aught that passed between the lovers.

"Why art thou delaying so long, my hero? all my life is slipping from me while thou tarriest. Surely twice thy summons came to me; meet me by the rock of plighted vows when I have called thee once again; and my life is slipping from me before thou callest. Oh! make haste, make haste."

"Ah! my lady, greatly loved and longed for, life-blood flows too slowly, something holds me that I cannot die and come to thee—a ringing in my ears of strange noises, like a noise of rowers, rowing on a water undergound, and still ascending—a noise of innumerable bells, that answer one another, from cliff and hill and valley; what meaning is herein I know not; if no answer comes, nor counsel, before sunrise, I will come."

"Alas, my hero, for my heart is breaking even now, and I shall stand upon the melancholy shore alone."

In the hearing of her ladies did she speak, "Let some one stand upon the walls and watch for the coming of the sun, and when the hills are rimmed with light, let her come before me." So one went and stood as she commanded. "Bring me now the book of Baldur, that is written in golden runes, which Engeltram, my lord, gave me on that day;" and another brought it, and sat at her feet to read therefrom, and read for a long space about the youth and beauty and holiness of Baldur, the Son of the All-Father, the beloved among the gods; and of the Evil Spirit Loki, how he conspired against Baldur, and caused him to be slain by his own friend, with the wood of that accursed branch, the mistletoe. So Baldur died, neither could any help be found for him; all the gods in Asgard wept for him, but could not save him. She read, moreover, that he departed in a burning ship, and should yet come again and visit men; and ever in that old mythology had it seemed most beautiful to Irminhilda and to Engeltram, that Baldur should come again. And the maiden sitting there, went reading on, but looked not upwards; yet she thought the morning air was strangely cold, and a shiver more than once went through her. Then she that had been watching on the wall, came in and stood before her mistress, saying, "My lady, in a moment the sun will rest upon the hills.—Hush! she is asleep, my lady;" and they kept silence before the figure as it seemed to sleep; but a long way off upon the coast, by the rock of plighted vows, stood the real Irminhilda, waiting for her lord.

Engeltram turned, and spoke unto the lords that stood round about him: "This day I go a long journey on the sea. Let, therefore, a ship be made ready and set for launching, and when I am dead, let me be carried to the shore in my rent armour as I lie, and with the sword of my achieving with me, and there lay me in the ship, looking westward; and so soon as the first wind comes from the sun, set me adrift upon the sea, and set the ship on fire, after the manner of the ancient kings, for this night I rest in Asgard, the city of the great gods." This he said as words they might understand, for he knew well concerning Asgard and Valhalla that they were not as his people thought, but his breath so failed him that he could not tell them, dying so, and he trusted one would come and teach them after his departure: —and once again a sound of measured dipping of the oars.

"Who shall steer thee into Asgard?" said the warriors; every man among them asked, "Let me steer thee into Asgard, in the burning ship."

Then said Engeltram, "I go not from you alone, but unseen hands shall steer me duly."

All the warriors said, each of them, "Let us row thee in the burning ship." But Engeltram shook his head mournfully, and answered, "Who should then protect this people, and give them laws, and teach them wisdom? they have no king, nor any to rule them. I go this day to enquire for them of the All-Father, that he may send them some one, either king or prophet, who shall lead them right. Do, therefore, as I have required of you, and when I am out of sight, watch stedfastly upon the shore until an answer come; for it will come." So they wept, and said that it should be so.

And after this, Engeltram smiled a happy smile, and seemed as if he were again listening, and one who kneeled and leaned over him, heard him muttering, "Yes, the same sound, nearer than before." Then he closed his eyes, and everywhere was silence; and the sun shot up above the ridge of eastern mountains; in a moment all the valley was lighted up with orient colours, also the helmets and brazen shields of the warriors were gilded with the beams that shot afar off, striking the four towers of the castle of Elstein. Then Engeltram shouted with the noise of a battle-cry, with a victorious shout: "The morning is come; very soon I shall be with you, Irminhilda." And the morning had come, and all the night and twilight ceased for ever.

"He is dead, he is dead." But they wept no longer; for the spoken words of the dead die not, but are everliving, and who knows the risk of disobedience, or whether it was a human voice only that spoke in them? They laid him, therefore in the ship, covering him with costly draperies, in his own broken armour, with his own good sword; and the chief among them took a firebrand, and lighted the helm; and the ship went off into the deep sea, blown by the early morning winds, steadily, swiftly onwards, burning like a setting sun: as the sun dies daily in a flame of fire along the west—as the whole world together shall yet die, consumed with fire, so was his passing out of life. All along the shore, whosoever had survived the battle, with the women and the children, gathered out of every house, watched it nearing the dark sea-line, looking for some wonder to happen.

On the margin of the water and the sky there shot up from it a momentary blaze of light high into heaven, and immediately after that it went down out of sight, either beyond the visible limit of the sea, or down below, sunk into its depths: then there was silence for a little space, neither did any dare to speak, remembering his last words and the promise that he gave them; in their hearts was deep anxiety. "Will Odin come?" thought they; "himself or Baldur, the White God. Oh! if Baldur would come and teach us!"

And therewithal it seemed to the farthest seers that the ship was returning to them from the under-world; and while they watched, it came nearer, nearer; and the sun behind them lighted up the ship, and revealed it full of men, white like spirits. "It is Baldur!" said the people. And the rowers in that strange vessel never rested from their labour till the fore part struck upon the sand and pebbles of the shore. "Surely it is Baldur!" said the people. He whom they so named bore a cross, and as he stepped upon the ground, there he planted it, deep into the yellow sand: on all the warriors and the old men and children there was silence. Very calm and holy was the face of the leader; like the face of Engeltram, long and thin and dark; his great white robe fell ungirdled in heavy and mighty folds to the feet: all this saw the people, observed the strange resemblance to their lost hero, and were silent.

Then he spoke to them; all day long he spoke and stayed not, true and credible tidings of Asgard. Like a starving people waiting for food did they stand and listen; none stepped aside or looked aside all that day. He spoke to them of life hereafter, of the love of the All-Father, till the eyes of the children and women were overcharged with tears; till the hearts of all the men were strong and brave. He spoke of the White God, and called him Christ.

The everlasting sun looked out upon them through spaces of great mountain-clouds, like a painted glory on a field of blue, passed behind the clouds, declined, and sank: all the pathway by which the burning ship had gone and the strangers come, lay upon the water like a molten golden pavement. Then came all the people and stepped into the bright water some few paces, and the sun went down, gazing as though it would yet linger, looking at the baptism of a nation; sinking swiftly at the last, as it would say, "I must visit other lands, but quickly I will come again to look;" for all the land was Christian.

Thus Engeltram fulfilled his promise, died and sent a prophet to them: and to all his memory was lovely; children also in the after-time heard his name sounded musically in all songs and ballads, and poets in that land saw oftentimes in their sweet dreaming Engeltram and Irminhilda on the other shore beyond the sea, walking hand in hand together, watching how the people fared.

Herewith I closed the volume. As if the distance across which I looked had made all speech inaudible, the lives of men in that far-off time came to me only in pictures: I could not hear them speak as they really spoke, could not know them as they were, but, just as when a friend has parted from us with whom we have held happy converse, and is now a long way behind upon the verge of land and sky, though we cannot hear him speak, yet do we none the less turn many times to look at him, yet is he none the less our friend whom we love, and his form traced upon the sky colossally we know and dwell upon. So was it with me. This book holds somewhere a page of crimson lettering, opaline and azure; on a summer day, when all the sky is laughing with merry blue, and the round shield of the sun burns in golden splendour, I will come again and open to that page, and read a story coloured like it, with love and laughter and happy issue; for the sequel of this first day's thought has left me, as it found me, sad; only somehow the great grey clouds and dark sea and mournful wind would flow to no other music than to sadness.

A Night in a Cathedral

By William Fulford

Late in the summer, or you may call it early in the autumn, a few years ago, I was making, unaccompanied, a pedestrian tour in the north-west of France. One of the first places I visited was Amiens, where I arrived on the afternoon of a bright sunny day. I almost immediately went to the Cathedral, in which I spent an hour and a half before dinner at the Table d'Hôte. Knowing very little about the technicalities of architecture, I will not attempt to give a description of the church, but will only say that I had never seen such entire loveliness in all my life. Since that time I have seen many cathedrals, in Germany and Italy, as well as in France, some of which are perhaps to be placed before this at Amiens; but it still remains in my memory with a peculiar tenderness,—something like the first love of childhood, which the loves of manhood can never efface. Almost immediately after the Table d'Hôte I returned to it. By this time the sun had set, and the short twilight rapidly died away. The Cathedral was to me now a totally different place from what it had been in the broad sunshine. I had examined it carefully and minutely before

dinner, and thus I now had a considerable knowledge of its details, which were every moment becoming dimmer and dimmer,
one after another fading altogether out of my sight. And now the
influence of the place stole over me, growing stronger and
stronger as the darkness increased. While I could see the rose
windows, and could make out distinctly the tracery and the
stained glass—the exquisite figures of the stone carvings in the
choir aisles—the stilted arches of the apse, and the carving of the
stalls—the building had been so beautiful that I felt no awe of it,
nothing graver than love. I even took pride in it as a glorious
work of man, nay, felt vain myself that I was a man also, like
those who had planned and built this miracle of beauty. But, in
the solemn twilight, in the deepening darkness, I saw farther and
more truly; I saw it as a house of God, and all my pride was
bowed down, and I was filled full of awe and humility. I paced
up and down the aisles: I passed chapel after chapel, kneeling
before which I could dimly see hundreds of people, scattered
throughout the vast space. I walked softly, almost on tiptoe,
fearing to disturb them, and feeling some shame, or, at the least,
regret, that I was not praying with them. I passed the awful light
in the chapel of the Blessed Sacrament: the painted glass was
faintly illumined, adding to the solemnity, with its pure holy colour. Light after light came out in the immense expanse; the feet
of French people, walking with more familiarity in their own accustomed church than I, a stranger, echoed from time to time.
Every now and then the shutting of a door reverberated with a
hollow but musical sound, and, scattering the stillness for a moment, the next moment made it still deeper. And for a few minutes I heard voices chaunting, far off, I knew not where; perhaps
in a Lady Chapel attached to the Cathedral. They were scarcely
audible; heard, even so faintly, only because of the depth of the
silence. The magic of their sweetness is beyond all power of
words to tell. In the hope of hearing them better, I sat down on
one of the many rush-bottomed chairs in the nave, looking up
towards the choir. They soon ceased, but I still sat, looking
through the rood-screen, at the apse, of which I could see very
little distinctly now. I did not care much for that; so well had its
details been impressed on my memory; though at times it was

painful to distinguish so little, the grandeur and extent so over-powered me and weighed me down. The night darkened, and still I sat or walked. The people present went away gradually, and fewer and fewer came in their stead, till at length I could see no one in the whole church. I did not know what time it was, having no watch with me, and not having heard a clock strike. I guessed it was about nine, and I expected that the Cathedral would soon be closed; but I was loth to leave it until the very moment when the doors should be shut. I waited, as it seemed, about a quarter of an hour, without seeing any one, or hearing any human sound. So comforting myself with the intention of returning in the morning, and going into the choir, and up into the triforium, and the tower and spire, I walked with reluctant steps to the south door, by which I had entered. It was fast; so I went to the door at the west end, but found that closed too. Upon this I walked to the north, but was greatly disconcerted to find the entrance there blocked up. With much quicker steps I went back to the west door and tried it again; shook it, pushed it, examined it as minutely as I could in the darkness—but all in vain. With increased trepidation I returned to the south door, trying to calm myself by the thought, that it was the one most likely to be open, and that I had tried it at first somewhat carelessly. I examined it more carefully than even the west door, but equally in vain. I was now really alarmed; so I walked, some-what slowly, round the whole church, looking out keenly and anxiously for another door. I walked completely round twice, but found no exit; there were only the doors leading to the towers. There was no longer room for doubt; I was shut up in the church by myself. I can scarcely tell what was my first feeling on this discovery. Often the first emotion on the reception of startling news is almost the very worst representative of the mul-tiplicity of feelings which it will afterwards from time to time occasion. Intelligence, the effect of which has been strong upon one for years afterwards, in the various phases of anger, grief, remorse, regret, at the time of receiving it, has left me almost as it found me—with the mind, doubtless stunned by the sudden-ness of the blow—only a little flurried, and unable to think con-secutively, and this excitement rather giving pleasure than pain.

And so this night I cannot say what feeling was predominant when I first discovered that I was shut up alone in so awful a place. Which came first? Was it terror, or a sort of sentimental pleasure, or resolution, or simple regret? I cannot tell; for a few seconds perhaps none at all very strongly or decidedly; or rather all were absorbed in, or more or less mixed with, surprise. But very soon they came, and for many long hours they stayed, feelings of such strength and acuteness as I have rarely experienced at other times even for a few minutes. My first thought was to try to sleep, both in the hope of thus passing the time in unconsciousness, and because I was very much tired. I placed three chairs side by side and lay down upon them. I had slept soundly many a time on a bed as hard; but I had not calculated upon the cold, which, when I came to keep still, I found intense.

After an interval of two or three years I cannot pretend to describe accurately the many mental phases which succeeded one another during this long night, the exact order in which they came, the strength with which they possessed me, least of all the precise length of time which they lasted. But there is much that I can recall with entire certainty, that I shall never forget till the day of my death. Some of these many feelings I will endeavour to describe, without any attempt at accurate chronology or minute analysis. My first emotion on finding that I could not go to sleep, was simple terror, which the sense of the darkness, while I had my eyes shut, had commenced. When a boy,—having been an imaginative and somewhat solitary child, reading much, and playing chiefly by myself—I had been a helpless prey to the fear of spirits—ghosts, hobgoblins,—all but fairies—and with not much love of them; and perhaps still more to the horror of the physical accompaniments of death. But, when I was fourteen years old, I began to attempt to control this terror, and had since so perseveringly excluded from my observation and reflection fearful sights and thoughts, that for the most part I held it in complete abeyance. But it was the safety rather of one who flies, and escapes for the time, than of one who fights and overcomes once and for ever. I felt, I feel even now, that if I were suddenly brought before some very terrible thing—I say it with full

belief—I even fear I should go mad. So now, all alone in darkness, in what seemed the dead of night, though probably it was
not ten o'clock, in a place so fearful as a church, with the dead
beneath my feet, and with spirits appearing to hover all round
me—all the old fear and horror rushed back upon me, and
seized me wholly, utterly powerless against them. The skeletons
rose from beneath the stones—thin, white ghosts glided before
me; the fiends in the tympanum, and from under the feet of the
saints, thronged into the church, and menaced me; the gargoyles
followed them, and played uncouth antics all about me, on the
floor, in the triforium, in the stalls—mowing and grimacing at
me. I heard their hideous half-human cries distinctly, mingled
with the rattling of the bones of the skeletons. In a few minutes,
after the first shock, Reason came to my aid. I need not record
her arguments, everybody could guess them, and everybody, like
myself, would have found no relief from them. Presently Imagination succeeded her, with a little more success—telling me that
I was not in a common church, with a graveyard round it, but in
a glorious Cathedral, the centre, as it were, of the living town;
that the dead, who lay beneath my feet, were not ordinary men,
but heroes and saints, buried here as a great honour and
privilege, sanctified themselves, and adding sanctity to their
resting-place; that above the fiends stood angels and holy men,
treading upon them in triumph. These thoughts somewhat miti-
gated my fear, but were far from charming it altogether away.

But now that it had once been checked, I summoned up all my
resolution to keep it down. I looked out boldly into the darkness,
and tried to fill up the details of the architecture, as I had seen
them in the daylight. In such a multitude of beauties it is hazardous to say what had most impressed and delighted me; but if I
were to select anything, it would be the stone-carvings in the
aisles of the choir, representing, on one side the history of St.
John the Baptist; on the other the history of a Bishop, I presume
a Bishop of Amiens. I had been particularly struck by the calm
pure beauty of some of the faces; and now, standing before these
carvings in the darkness, I tried to recall those countenances, to
still the tumult of my dread by their heavenly repose. They came

out from the blankness, but with partial distinctness; after a little while passing off into foul and ugly faces, of demons and wicked men, which increased my fright.

Upon this I attempted to realize the performance of Mass in the Cathedral. I had not yet heard Divine service in France, and had but a very vague conception of the grand and beautiful music which in a little while I heard in the Cathedrals of Beauvais, Chartres, and Rouen. I had heard the Roman Catholic service performed a few times in England, and had been greatly impressed by its splendour and pathos; but I had no idea how the Mass and Vespers, as celebrated in these French churches, range rapidly through every variety of feeling;—now a solemn simple Gregorian chaunt, presently a solo on the organ, bowing the hearer prostrate with its pathos;—now organ and choir bursting out in a loud song of triumph, as if for some victory just won over the powers of evil, which anon subsides into a strong but melodious strain of calm joy, like the angels singing in their undisturbed bliss of eternity. Accordingly, I guided myself chiefly by the remembrance of Mozart's Requiem, which I had heard performed at Exeter Hall; but both from this circumstance and from the influence of the darkness, my mass became a Service for the dead: the organ played a mournful prelude; I heard the sorrowful *De Profundis* sung by bass voices to a Gregorian chaunt; then a priest intoned words which I could not understand, till suddenly it seemed that the whole choir of the church was filled with a huge orchestra and chorus, which thundered forth with stern sublimity, as I had actually heard in the *Dies Iræ* of the Requiem, that fearful cry of self-condemned humanity:

> "Quantus tremor est futurus,
> Quando Judex est venturus,
> Cuncta stricte discussurus!"

As I have said before, I cannot pretend to accuracy in this account, and accordingly I do not know whether what I am about to describe came next in order or not. I set myself to work to call back the times in which the Cathedral was built, and to summon up before me its builders and its earliest congregations. I knew nothing of its history, except that its date might be placed generally in the thirteenth century. I knew also very little of the Middle Ages; but I could not help knowing enough to picture vague figures of bishops and priests in rochet and cope, knights in chain armour, crusaders with the cross on their left shoulder, among them the holy Louis with his beautiful, devoted face, and his companion in arms, our own Edward, with his loving brave wife Eleanor, and, by association, the Lion-hearted king, the most stalwart of them all, whose very name passed into a word of terror among the Saracens.

I saw also the masons at work on the statues, while others of the guild painted the frescoes; and in the midst of them the architect himself, whose name I knew not, whose name, it may be, the world is equally ignorant of, such is the caprice of fame; the chief designer of this grandeur and beauty, but himself a workman like the rest, a master mason. I saw him carving a statue in the tympanum, the Virgin Mary, whose face grew beneath his hands with such pure loveliness as I had never seen in face before, either in art or in actual life. And next him was a young man, who perhaps was his favourite pupil, placing a female saint on the back of a devil, which was already fixed up in the porch, crouching down helplessly, though with defiance in his looks; but before the saint's feet could be set upon him, he leapt down from his place, and gambolled into the church; and, oh horror! he was followed by a host of devils and gargoyles; and the stern knights and sad priests rose from their graves, skeletons with armour and robes dangling and folding about them, making the night hideous beyond endurance.

All my courage was beaten down; I rushed to the west door; I shook it with all my force, I struck it with both my fists, I hurled my weight frantically against it, but no answer came, except hollow reverberations, after which the stillness deepened tenfold. It was beyond the power of man to bear; I shrieked aloud! fool, fool that I was, who could hear me? only frightful echoes of my own voice mocked the wild cries of my senseless anguish.

Then my frantic violence suddenly gave way, but only to a quieter kind of despair, and I burst into tears, sitting down on the tomb of a knight that is placed at the west end. But by this time fortunately I had become very sleepy, and despite the cold I fell into a doze, which came to me at first as a most welcome relief. But soon my terror pursued me into my sleep, and brought up before me visions which I had not seen since I was a boy, lying ill of sick headache. It seemed that I was in some place unutterably vast, which at one time appeared the Cathedral, at another time vaster even than the earth itself. But huge as it was, it kept pitilessly growing on every side, higher, deeper, wider; I say pitilessly, for there was a personality in the inanimate objects of my dreams, which was perhaps their greatest torment. Then I felt myself in the presence of awful, cold beauty,— inexpressibly lovely, but with no love for me. It was as if some old friend had proved false, or as if I had hitherto mistaken my own nature, and aimed at that which was too high for me. How miserable, how degraded I felt! I could see the beauty, but could not feel it,—at least not as I had felt it of old, when it was almost unmixed delight to me; but now I could only feel fear, not mere awe of it, and I had lost a power which I had thought would never leave me,—which seemed my life, my essence, my very self.

Then I was standing in the midst of friends, and we were together, talking softly and tenderly; but suddenly, in a second, I stood, I know not how carried thither, on an island, alone,—of immense size it seemed, with a limitless ocean rolling round it,—yet, far off, at an infinite distance, I could see myriads of men and women, in the world, and could catch, how faintly and mournfully, the hum of their voices as they talked together. What agony of desolation! Separated from all for ever, to be a far-off spectator of men, a listener to the sound, the sound only, of their voices! I awoke starting, and opened my eyes, but only upon the intolerable blackness. Like a solid wall it stood round me on every side. I seemed in the heart of a rock, of a mountain; buried, but in worse than a tomb, with its cold obstruction of earth; buried in darkness, in darkness which might be felt, which closed me in, and would not let me stir. I lay motionless, in an agony of stillness; for I felt myself, for a few seconds, literally unable to move.

I was still very sleepy, and probably passed great part of the night in a state of drowsiness; but the cold, which, while it cruelly

ate into my body, yet in some measure befriended me by drawing off my attention from my mental suffering, would not permit
me to sleep, or even to stand still long together. Motion on the
one hand diverted my fear; but on the other hand it had its
peculiar terrors. It was while I was moving that the fear of the
darkness was the greatest. It seemed to present an impassable
barrier to my advance; sometimes it seemed itself to advance
against me, threatening to devour me: at times it was full of all
horrible things, but generally it was mere void blankness, more
fearful, I think, than even when it seemed alive with demons and
foul beasts. But yet greater was the dread of passing the doors
that lead to the towers. The terror, yet fascination, of these was
beyond description. I had rarely gone up into towers, and they
were as yet a mystery to me: a belfry was as strange and dreadful
a place to me as a vault. But to this was now added the immense
height of the Cathedral: I felt the well-known longing to throw
myself down from it, and it seemed as if, in the utter darkness,
could I have ascended the tower, and got on to one of the
parapets I could not have resisted the spell. I say as I walked by
those doors I was in positive alarm for my life: my will was
thoroughly weakened, quite broken by terror, agitation, and
want of sleep: I had no power to prevent myself from passing by
the doors, neither could I make head against the desire of entering one of them and mounting to the parapet. In this agony,
one thought alone comforted me; the belief, the almost certain
assurance, that the doors would be locked. So, half with this expectation, to put an end to my fascination, half in obedience to it,
I tried the locks. Thank God! it was as I had expected; they were
fast. And thus the long hours went on, and still the darkness
continued. I could stretch my account to much greater length by
waiting till memory should give substance and continuity to
those shadowy fragments which are now floating in my mind. I
might tell how strangely the symbolical character of the Gothic
architecture affected me, though I knew little of the symbolism;
at one time relieving me by engaging my mind in an attempt to
understand its meaning; at another time deepening my fear by
its mysteriousness. Or I might attempt to describe, more at
length and with more accuracy, my physical sensations, the ef-

fects of the cold, of the dampness, of the fatigue, of the want of sleep, of the faint hunger that every now and then reminded me that I had eaten nothing since six o'clock the preceding evening. But I must draw to a close, telling only of the last stage of my sufferings, when the morning at length came to end them. Grey and dreary, it broke very slowly, for some time only darkness visible; and little by little the tracery of the windows, and the stone carvings, and the capitals of the pillars, were given back from the gloom. How different they seemed now, in this desolate dawn, and yesterday, when I first beheld them, in the brightness of the afternoon sun. For the morning, a little while back so eagerly longed for, now, when it was come, was almost as unwelcome as the night. I have never in all my life besides felt such profound sadness as now while this dawn was slowly brightening. Alone in a foreign country, shut up in a church, the ghostly twilight shimmering in through stained glass,—I was prostrated in utter dejection. It seemed that all the sorrows of my life rose to my mind, which, by its very weariness, was unable to control its thoughts,—sorrows which in the active day had not risen from their tombs for months and years; above all, the great sorrow which for a time had made the earth, a garden before, a very wilderness to me. I saw faces which I had not looked upon for years; faces of the dead,— and, sadder still, faces of the changed; these last, coming sometimes with the smile of the kinder, earlier time, sometimes with the cold look of estrangement; my living friends also passed before me, but with looks how different from their own! None laughing, — a few smiling, but sorrowful smiles,—and one or two were weeping; and I listened, and the voices were changed, and it seemed a voice, once heard how often, and still remembered how vividly, sobbing, and, amid its sobs, brokenly uttering my own name,—a voice which I had never heard weep, but which I had often thought must have wept bitterly many times over lost love.

At last, at last, the key turned in the lock of the south door, and the world was open to me again; but I walked to the entrance leisurely, almost listlessly, too far exhausted to feel much joy at my deliverance.

The Rivals

By R. W. Dixon

I have a wish to record the master-facts of my life—facts not
the less real and important, to myself at least, because the joys
and sorrows of which they are composed are difficult to be set
forth in words, to be separated from the unformed quarry of
feelings and half-thoughts. They are what has given me, who am
poor and unknown, memories for the sake of which I would not
change my identity with that of the brightest genius, and hopes
which are full of the life which is "the life indeed"—the life of
revived death. Oh the malignity of that first devil's lie—"Ye shall
not surely die!" Surely, surely everything here points to death as
the path of life. They who have slain their ambition, their selfish
hopes, their passions, these are the conquerors who are "dead,"
and whose life is "hid with Christ in God." But let me go on to say
how a nature strong and passionate, while scorning what is false
and base, was yet long in attaining aught that is true and pure.

I am not particularly remarkable for anything. The prevailing
quality which I have observed in myself being a very great degree (so I consider it) of *impressibleness*, which has had the effect

of making me very shy and reserved. My observation during the first part of my life fell upon men rather than upon nature, owing to a peculiar education. For I am constitutionally very delicate; was sent to school late, and passed all my school-days in my native place, one of the largest manufacturing towns in England. True it is that I have watched many times the smoke-drifts rushing swiftly across the streets, pursuing and pursued, with shapes more quickly changing, fiercer and more fantastic than those of the slow white clouds above them; true that I have seen the half-filled pools of the brick-field, which, poor and contemptible though they are, bear often upon them the floating moon, their one white flower, swell and brim into vast and boundless lakes, point after point receding into lofty mountains, clothed with woods and based with half-seen towers: true that I have seen the great sun sink over the town into a bank of vapours, above which curled and writhed and flew the everlasting smoke, so that I have thought of many things to which that sunset might be likened: true that I have fancied the long rows of poplars and aspens which I sometimes visited outside the town, beyond the brick-field, and which seemed stiff with for ever twisting themselves from the killing smoke, and which rattled when the wind was upon them; true, I say, that I have fancied these beloved suffering trees to be swaying white and green, with a million bright glancings, in some golden country where the sun should shine always, and the wind blow always warm and soft. All this, and more of the same sort, is true; but I got no further. I had but little opportunity for any accurate knowledge of nature, and but few of the now familiar changes and sounds, in which I have since found my purest delight, fell upon my senses in boyhood. The dragons in the smoke, the mountains, woods and castles of the brick-pools, the images of sun and sunset, the waving trees, and happy country, were stored safely up in my imagination among its chief treasures, to be recurred to again and again. There they were, and to me were an unfailing possession, along with a golden harp which I had seen when very young, and the head of an angel, beheld once in a picture and never forgotten. But men became my chief study, and it was my great delight to watch the faces that passed me in the street, framing for each a

history and character suited to what I fancied was their expression. Among my school-fellows I was liked, being considered,
though very shy, yet anxious to please. This was indeed true, and
the worse for. Speculation upon others implied, of course, a
continual comparison of others with myself; and, being joined
with a natural timidity, or, as I have called it, impressibility,
whilst it gave me considerable insight into character, rendered
me, above all things, desirous to adapt myself to the different
people into whose society I was thrown. Thus was formed in me,
almost from the beginning, a dangerous habit of self-introspec-
tion, and a nervous wish to give pleasure at any cost; wherein was
involved a want of moral courage, and a positive selfishness,
which might easily turn the first calamity into morose despairing,
or sully the first love with turbid passion.

Being then such an one, reserved, timid, and, though I knew it
not, selfish, I removed, at the usual age, to the University. It
should be added, that at this time I was fond of poetry, a poet,
and cherishing an almost insane pride in my art and confidence
in my power. This contributed to my shyness and taciturnity,
and I fear to my selfishness. At the University I renewed my
acquaintance with Arnetage, a young man whom I had known at
school, and who had quitted school a year before myself. Arnetage is dead now, and so is *she*; and it is well, for death alone could
measure the love wherewith I loved them both.

In no long time my acquaintance with Arnetage deepened into
true and lasting love. I loved him for his beauty, his intellect, his
spendid temper, his everlasting cheerfulness. He loved me too, I
know not why; but so it was, that surrounded by the brilliant and
the gay, himself the most brilliant and the gayest, he turned to
quiet timid me, and sought to make me his friend. We read together Keats and Tennyson, to the latter of whom he introduced
me. I remember thinking that his admiration for Tennyson
savoured rather of dilettanteism, that he was rather taken by the
melody of the verse, than possessed by the power and glory of
the divine poet. He used to express his rapture in words; I sat in
silence and enjoyed; and I thought that, because he could only
express a little of what I felt within myself, that his appreciation
was less deep and fine than my own. It did not occur to me, so

enthusiastic did he seem in what he was saying, that perhaps he also felt something which he did not express, because it was beyond the power of expression. I was slow in finding out that his soul was infinitely deeper, truer, and tenderer than my own. He could have done unfalteringly what I should have failed to do in repeated and bitter struggles.

But there was friendship, and more than friendship between us. He told me the history of his whole life, a tale of heroic habitudes, gentle and self-forgetful; told in such an unconscious way, that I also forgot while listening to mark its nobleness, feeling as if he were myself. Amongst other things, he related how he had been from a boy betrothed to his cousin Margaret, who lived in our town with her widowed father and a maiden aunt: how he had rebelled against this betrothal with his whole soul, had seen Margaret for a long time only to dislike her, but at length had been so won upon by her beauty and her perfect mind, that his dislike had changed to love: how, a few months before I knew him at college, he had declared to Margaret his scruples and his love: how Margaret had owned at once the same scruples, ending in the same love. All this did he pour into my wondering ear, so that I listened as to a revelation, eagerly longing to experience the same blessedness. For then I knew not love—that mightiest magician, who can lift man to heaven or sink him into hell. At the end of three years Arnetage left the University, and I saw no more of him for a long time. The only fault, if fault it can be called, which I had seen in him was an extreme delicacy, a haughty and absolute withdrawal into himself at the slightest symptom of neglect or misapprehension.

At the end of my own career at the University I returned to my native town, which was, as I have said, one of the largest in England. And now comes the grand incident of my life. I was walking one day in one of the suburbs, where I had not often been, for it was divided by the greatest extent of the town from the part where I lived myself. It was an uncertain day, towards the close of autumn; there seemed a mist of light about the clouds; it was raining in the distance, but sometimes the sun broke forth irregularly, drawing northward across the fields long shadows of chestnut and poplar, and striking the red bricks of the nearer houses into vivid light. A large house, with its garden in front, at the end of a short street into which I turned, was thus struck by the sunlight as I began to approach it. In the midst of the sudden brightness, the flower shrubs and glittering trees of the garden, my eyes fell upon a form which instantly fascinated their gaze: it was the form of a lady—a face perfectly beautiful, the eyes uplifted in joyful surprise towards the sudden light, the rich dark hair glowing a purple beneath the sun, the white dress radiant. The look was of surprise and pleasure, but did not dissipate the tokens of tranquil power and dignity which I immediately understood would be the usual expression. I approached in breathless eagerness. No one else was in the street, and I longed, I knew not why, to be nearer. I wished my footsteps were noiseless as I went crashing along the wet gravel; but, as I reached nearly opposite, without apparently perceiving me, the beautiful vision slowly withdrew, and at the same instant the sunlight suddenly was swept away.

It did not strike me then, nor for many months after, that the quarter of the town where this circumstance occurred was the same in which Arnetage had told me that his cousin lived. But I found that the angel's face, which was even yet among the most cherished possessions of my imagination, had faded, or changed, and become identified with the beautiful presence in the garden. I found myself indescribably affected by that face. I thought of nothing else. I talked to that image in murmurous words. I fancied the beautiful unknown in various situations of peril and difficulty, in which I was to appear the rescuer. I was, and am, poor; and at the time in question, was very proud, indeed morbidly sensitive on the subject of money. She, I concluded, from what I had seen, must be comparatively wealthy. I am ashamed to have to say that it cost me a struggle to imagine myself even in that poor way dependent upon her, whom I now felt that I loved with all the passion of my nature, and to whom I hoped one day to owe all the happiness of my life. Never did lover feel more hopelessly the curse of poverty than I did. I summoned round her in imagination, trembling the while with apprehension, whole troops of wealthy and fortunate suitors, legions of tempters, matchmakers and formalists,—round her, who, as I found it hard to realize, was ignorant of my very existence; while the only consolation for my mingled pride and terror was to see her imaginarily cast down from wealth, deserted by the world, and discovering me the only faithful. I mention this that you may perceive to what I was reduced by passion, which could find no issue, self-corroding and hopeless.

I can well recall the second visit I paid to that neighbourhood. The interval between that and the first was brief, if measured by time—but how long measured by what I had felt. The day was just such another as before; bursts of sunshine, alternated with slender rain, each seemingly wafted from the silken sulky clouds in joyous contradiction by the same wind. How I approached the house, expecting to see the same transfiguring light, the same sweet happy face, and head "sunning over with curls." How I was disappointed, as matter of course, seeing nothing but the house-roof shining with rain, the wet trees and garden railing, and the blank windows! How I slunk away, wondering whether any one had been watching me from those same windows, and whether this any one (who took form in my mind as a violently timid aunt) would not take me for an inspectant housebreaker. Throughout that winter I found myself doing the same thing. It was the only course my passion could shape for itself. Night and day, in sunshine and rain, but oftenest when evening had set in, and the gas-lights of the suburb glimmered few and far between, each in its halo of fog, and the lights of the houses shone behind the blinds, and so, until these lights disappeared and re-appearing above, were finally extinguished, was I to be seen, pacing about and about,with a fire at my heart, an anguish, and a longing irrepressible, that sometimes amounted to positive physical pain. This was my great time, for, during the day, I felt conscious, and guilty, and ashamed; and, after walking the whole town's length, through mire and thawing snow, for the sole purpose of getting a glimpse of the place where she might be, I would pass meekly by, scarcely raising my eyes, and feeling more than ever like a housebreaker—a fancy which I could not get out of my head. I had no means of getting an introduction to the family, though I attempted it repeatedly. My sole reward for my walks and vigils was a very occasional glance of her face at window or door, and once I was nearly in time to see her enter the gate; and once I met her in the town, and once saw her in a carriage driving along a road leading into the country, which road was forthwith added to my dreary beat. These were rare intervals of brightness, and served to urge into fiercer heat the fire which was consuming my life. When I reflected on what I was enduring, I sometimes thought myself actually mad, and, in fact, my strange self-tortures may have had insanity in them.

Thus the winter wore lingeringly away. In the spring, Arnetage returned from a tour on the Continent, in which he had been engaged ever since I left college. A little time before his return, I had grown desperate, and had concocted a notable scheme for gaining access to the abode of the unknown. From the door-plate, I had long ago ascertained that the family name was Stuart, and heard one day accidentally, from a picture-dealer, that Mr. Stuart possessed a picture that was the pride of the town. Now, I had some skill in judging of pictures, and my opinion was held of value. Could I not call with my friend the picture-dealer, for the purpose of inspecting the picture? Perhaps he did not know Mr. Stuart; perhaps his Mr. Stuart and mine were different individuals; perhaps, as had already been the case with many such a scheme of mine, I should not venture to propose it at all. But just then I was full of it, meditating and resolving, when Arnetage stood before me.

He expressed himself shocked at my pale and altered looks, but soon seemed to forget them in an account of his travels and adventures, which he gave with delightful animation and humour. It was late when he rose to depart.

"Well," said he, giving me his hand, "I have cheered you up a little tonight; and to-morrow, to complete the healing process, I mean to introduce you to my beautiful betrothed, Margaret Stuart."

He had never mentioned her name before.

"Margaret Stuart," said I, "why I thought her name was Arnetage."

It was all over. A dulness, a torpor, almost a swoon, had fallen upon me, after Arnetage's departure, during the time when my mind refused to contemplate the greatness of my misfortune. I had found that my best beloved friend was my rival, that was all that I could realize; but this dull torpor was penetrated, shot through by sharpest pangs, and these gradually increased in intensity and frequency until I awoke to my situation, as I have often been awaked from an actual sleep by bodily pain. And now began a long and terrible struggle of love, pride, jealousy, and friendship, which lasted throughout the hours of darkness. As the sun's rim appeared, I at length slept, thinking that I had conquered myself by coming to the following resolution; that no one should ever know of my love; that I would not even attempt to forget Margaret, but would love her still, and love her fervently and purely, even as I loved Arnetage; and that I would strive to find my happiness in witnessing the happiness of the two whom best I loved on earth, accustoming myself to love them for their love of one another. I awoke next morning from a heavy and troubled sleep, full of brave resolutions, and prayed fervently, as I had need. In those fiery hours of the preceding night, my old agonized love, in which I had writhed as in fire, seemed finally to have burned itself out. I shuddered at myself, when I thought of the past—of my mad self-torments. It seemed, indeed, like an evil, yet irresistibly fascinating dream. So, when Arnetage came to conduct me to the presence of his Margaret, I found myself full of virtue and self-pity; and, as it were, above him, on a little moral hill, wherefrom calmly to survey him, my unconscious rival, as he stood before me in his brightness, beauty, and strength. It was not very well, but it was all I could do, for my nature is feeble and passionate.

I went then, and stood face to face with the magnificent beauty, which I thought I knew so well. I saw the noble opulence of face and form, the commanding tranquillity, which I had pictured but too well; I heard the full measured tones of that sweet rich voice, and met the gaze of those large meditating eyes. I marked too the quiet love that was between them; how noble they both were, how calmly regardful of one another. Love, that had burst like an angry wave into my poor breast, had flowed without agitation into those vast and gulf-like hearts. I felt myself inconceivably insignificant. I looked at Arnetage serenely smiling, and found it hard to love him. In spite of everything, the old sore was reopening, the old wasting miserable agony was coming back. I took dim note of other things. There was furniture lavish and gorgeous; there was the picture—a portrait whose eyes followed me everywhere. There were also some other people in the room. A good-natured nervous old gentleman tried to talk to me. He was Margaret's father. An oldish, vixenish, foolishly acute-looking lady thought she was scrutinizing me closely. She was Margaret's aunt, and of her more hereafter.

On our way back, Arnetage asked me with anxious confidence what I thought of his cousin.

"Perfectly beautiful, and you ought to be very happy." I spoke bitterly and foolishly, for did not his broad-beaming smile speak of love, trust, and full happiness?

However, after a while I succeeded in recovering something of the resolutions of the morning. It was impossible to look upon the glorious being before me, so thoroughly possessed by his own love, and yet so delicately kind and affectionate to me, and regard him with an eye of spleen or envy. And I thought, improbable as it seemed, that something might occur to cloud that sunny heaven of love. The thought was born of baseness; let me confess it, for I somehow drew from it consolation for my own despair; but oh! love so faultily passionate as mine is very dangerous when brought suddenly to hopelessness. The thought did good by arousing at once all my friendship for Arnetage. I recollected the one weakness of his character, which seemed strangely inconsistent with the rest of it; the shrinking haughtiness which scorned vindication by words, and caused him to retire for ever on the slightest appearance of misapprehension or unworthy suspicion. And I disliked that old vixenish aunt, who, I felt, was totally incapable of comprehending the character either of Arnetage or of her niece, and who seemed to have great influence over her more quiet but equally shortsighted brother.

After this, I saw Arnetage daily. We renewed as much as possible our old college life. We read together, we walked together, we talked together. Arnetage, as I had discovered at college, was a poet, and had now produced a great number of pieces more or less finished, and we spent many happy hours in criticising and correcting these, deciding between various readings, amending rhymes, and reconstructing stanzas; occasionally engaged in eager debate. I had long since given up the dream of being a poet myself, but it gave me no pang of envy to see my friend nearing the goal which I could only behold afar off. Arnetage introduced me to his father—his mother was dead years ago—a fine specimen of the English merchant, frank and honourable, like his son; a keen judge of character, inured to the most vigorous and responsible exertions, full of benevolence and hospitality. He had raised himself to great opulence, and was enabled to achieve successfully, by dint of his own intuitive sagacity, the most hazardous speculations. His danger lay, in my opinion, in over confidence in his own resources: he was in the habit of risking everything on a die hitherto thrown with unerring skill. He was still actively engaged in commerce, and no one stood higher in the estimation of all men. I also now frequently saw Margaret, alone and with Arnetage, and at each interview felt a relapse, though fainter and fainter, into my old mad whirl of passion. Ah! it cost many bitter struggles with myself, with what I had exalted as the better, the saving part of my nature, many despairing cries to God, before I could completely master the old besetment, and love her not for myself but for him. But by degrees I conquered, and learned to love them both at once for their love to one another, even as I marked the still growth of that love of theirs, so frank, so utterly above caprice or concealment, or common passion. These things continued for a year, until Arnetage's book came out, bearing his name boldly on the title-page. And indeed I thought there was nothing in it to be ashamed of.

Now it came to pass that a certain great reviewer happened to be in want of a victim whose dissection should add a zest to his forthcoming number. What could be fairer game than the first book of a young poet, particularly of one who presumptuously dared to put his name upon his work, thereby doing despiteful defiance to the critical might, and offering the better mark for the critical arrows. Besides, the upstart pretended to high aspirations and imaginings, and, as the great reviewer had it, "manifested the usual spirit of restless discontent with the things that be," meaning to signify a certain unreasonable dislike to cant and tyranny and hypocrisy. So the great reviewer first attempted to classify, to catalogue, the book, and failing in that, perhaps even to his own dissatisfaction, fell upon it and rated it in good set terms, misunderstanding, misrepresenting—all but misquoting; and in this process gratuitously and scandalously insulting the author. The affair made me very indignant, and at first aroused the wrath of Arnetage, but after a time he forgave it, because, as he said, "pity was akin to forgiveness," and he even laughingly showed the article to Margaret, who had the poems by heart, and reverenced their author. About the time that this article appeared, a much more serious embarrassment befel Arnetage. The failure of a bank and the ill success of a great speculation, greatly involved the affairs, and even compromised considerably the commercial character of his father. Arnetage was obliged to apply himself vigorously to relieve the pressure of labour and anxiety which fell upon the old man.

The news that the great merchant's credit was tottering spread all over the town, and at length reached the ears of Mr. Stuart, to whom it occasioned no small disquiet. For the father of my friend had always been to Mr. Stuart an oracle and lode-star, and he had been wont to look with pride upon his future alliance with the Arnetages. To hear that he was falling shocked Mr. Stuart very greatly. He was however reassured after a personal interview with Mr. Arnetage. But the aunt, who had him very much under control, being perfectly incompetent to form a notion of the real state of things, and being a person of some imagination of a kind, immediately upon hearing the rumours in circulation, had a vision of Mr. Arnetage in the Court of Insolvency. How was this mental fact to bear upon the destinies of Margaret and my friend? The good lady might have become reconciled even to the dismal result she had conjured up, for she had discernment enough to see that Arnetage was vigorous and alert, and might raise a goodly structure of wealth even from the ruins of his father. And she had moreover a great veneration for literature, and had not Arnetage written a book? So she was not at all sure whether, considering the attachment which existed between her niece and Arnetage, it were not as well to let things take their present course, even in such dismal contingency as bankruptcy.

But at this critical point of her speculations, the review left at the house by my unlucky friend fell into her hands, and worked an instantaneous revolution. Behold what was thought of the provincial pretender in the orthodox capital of letters! Was not Arnetage a fool, an ignoramus, even as the great reviewer described him? She felt half shocked at having, as she thought, admired his poems, and remembered with comfort that it had cost her an effort to do so. And she rapidly proceeded to discover that she never had liked that young man, she always felt strange with him; there was something about him she never could get accustomed to. Finally she went forthwith to announce her impressions to Mr. Stuart, carrying the review with her.

Mr. Stuart was a good deal staggered, especially at the considerate estimate of his intended son-in-law in the review, for he, too, entertained the most unbounded reverence for printed words. He could not, however, all at once divest himself of the long habit of looking forward to the future alliance as a desirable thing; but his sister's incessant remonstrances so far succeeded in counterbalancing his usual good nature, that he managed the next time Arnetage came to give him a tolerably cool reception. This was enough for Arnetage, whose pride was then in an unusually active condition; he kept himself away from visiting the Stuarts for more than a fortnight, and then suddenly returned, and abruptly demanded that a day should be fixed for his union with Margaret. The reply from her father was courteous, to the effect that the marriage could not take place until present affairs were cleared up, and Arnetage was in some settled occupation. Margaret's heart flowed out towards her lover; she had been daily pestered about the review and the sinister reports afloat, and she fully understood and forgave his absence. He should marry her, she said, whenever he pleased, and even if the rumoured ruin of his father were true, still she had enough for both, and had confidence in his honour and industry. But when Arnetage decided otherwise, she obeyed. "It is better," he said, "for both of us that our marriage should be delayed; we can trust one another, for if not, let us never be married at all; it does not become us that anything should be done hastily. Your father's hint about my desultory mode of life may be true, and I will reform. My father's affairs require that a trusty agent should be sent into the Mediterranean, to examine the proceedings of certain rascally Italian and Levantine traders. I will go, and doubt not that in good time I shall return to claim you as mine by right of conquest."

So he went, I accompanying him to the water-side. We paced together the small and unfrequented pier, pending the arrival of the steamer, the sea-weed bulbs cracking beneath our feet; for it was his whim to embark not at Liverpool, but at one of the numerous villages further out towards the sea. Here I told him of my resolution to abide in Liverpool until he returned, adding, that I had already secured lodgings. He seemed surprised, and said, that he hoped nevertheless I should see Margaret often, and write to him all particulars about her. I promised this with eagerness; though alas, my real object in removing to Liverpool was to get away from the place where she was, for I mistrusted myself in his absence. I longed, for a moment, to tell him all that lay concealed within me, but now the mighty steamer was rapidly sweeping down along with the tide, which was fast running out. Arnetage and I sprang into our boat, and were soon alongside: another moment, and he was waving his hand to me from the steamer's deck, and I was sadly pulling back.

I found that not without reason had I mistrusted myself; even when Arnetage was with me, keeping alive by word and look my love for him, even then the selfishness in my breast had arisen again and again in opposition to the honourable course I strove to keep before me. And now he was gone, and I could see my soul's idol alone; alone I could behold those large and humid eyes, that to him used to kindle or to dissolve, raining, as it were, tears of light and love; and those lips that grew richer in pathos, with the answer that hung upon them when he spoke: I could listen alone to that voice which to him would vibrate with pride and tenderness. What if they should beam and melt, and vibrate to me at the mention of him? How could I dare, then, to see her? I saw her once, once only, and the consequences to me were awful. To avoid committing folly, I was compelled to leave her suddenly, and fling myself into the first railway train for Liverpool. And there I sat sad, depressed and trembling with the violent effort it had cost me to leave her presence. Every soaring bird, every tree and field, every house and church, which I thanked heaven that we rushed so quickly by, seemed to bear a message and remembrance from Margaret. In Liverpool my only comfort was to pace the little pier where Arnetage and I had stood, hearing the sea-weed burst beneath my feet, looking toward the sea and cloud, calling upon his name. Arnetage, Arnetage! Oh wild, wide, lone, and barren sea, and shadows untasted by the sun! were not ye even as the darkness over me, in which I struggled with cries and tears, stretching abroad blind hands of supplication.

I wrote to Arnetage twice, and heard from him once; he wrote from Greece, and said that he was about to sail for Italy. Margaret was well the second time I wrote.

A hasty message came to me that Margaret was suddenly and seriously ill. None knew what ailed her; some said she pined for Arnetage. I knew that she did not. Hers was not the love that had to do with pining and common regrets for absence. Did not her eye that one day kindle with joy and love to me at the mention of his name, as if he had been with her? But she grew thin, and weakened day by day. Perhaps the vessel was too full of love and happiness, and holy faith. But she weakened very swiftly, and the best thing people said of it was, that she was too good for this world. Indeed, she vanished more than died. As for me, it was enough, and too much, to pace the street in front of the house, as I used to do of old, looking constantly at the candle that burned all night behind the blind of her room; now bright, now dimmer, and again brighter, I paced about sternly and mechanically, thinking only of her, and of the loss to me; thinking of Arnetage only, with a dull sort of speculation as to the manner in which he would receive the news. The people of the house knew that I was there, and humoured me; sometimes coming out to tell me that she was better. At length some one came, and said that she wished to speak to me. In an instant the thought of Arnetage came upon my mind with full force, and I shuddered, actually dreading, lest I should profane that angel's death-bed with an outbreak of passion. I went, as if walking in a dream, into the parlour, where was the aunt weeping, and the father.

"Do you think," I began vacantly, "that she wishes to see me?"

"To be sure, that is what you have just been told," began the old man testily, hurriedly adding, "why good heavens, how ill you look!"

The next moment I had fallen heavily upon the floor. I came to my senses in a week, and found myself on my own bed, attended by my own old servant. I felt thankful for this, for if I had raved, perhaps no one had heard me. I have never asked. But the end had been reached; I found Margaret had expired the day before.

I visited her grave once, once only for many years. I dared not go again until long years had passed away. And this was the reason. I said to myself one morning, the first on which I found myself able to walk—this day I will go to the grave, but not yet. So I waited all that day, feeling horrible, and full of earthy power. I was obliged to see several people, and had often to put the strongest restraint upon myself lest I should scream and sob aloud. In the evening I went to the grave. It was in the suburb, not very far from my house, on the other side of the hill, whereon stood the long row of poplars turned in sickness from the reeking smoke that was withering them. The sun was setting on the other side of the town, as I had often watched him in my early days: the sun, I say, was setting, slipping down sadly into the dense smoke of the horizon, and casting sheets of pale yellow over the higher parts of the western sky. There was scarce another colour, until this sank into a bloody, ghastly, smoke-traversed region, wherein was the dying king of heaven himself. The cold gravestone was bathed in this pale yellow light, the freshly turned soil about was yellow and clayey, and mixed with trodden grass: it was autumn again, and the trees and paths were filled with yellow leaves. I moved about mournfully, mournfully; read the epitaph, looked long and sadly at the grave, thinking how much love she that lay below had awakened in me, and how she had died without knowing it. I came away resolved never to return, "for the sky will never be blue, nor the earth be happy, while I am by, and she will be troubled among the dead. She cannot be mine even in the grave. I will return no more."

I have said that Arnetage was to go to Italy, from his last letter.

I had written to him since, both when Margaret's illness came on, and when she grew worse and after her death. But no answer came. About three weeks after the funeral, I was sitting alone in my room, in Liverpool, reading the exquisite narrative of the death of Guy, in the *Heir of Redcliffe*. My tears were dropping fast, and I was half praying at times for peace and patience like Amy's. Suddenly I heard a step ascending to my room—a step which caused me, I knew not why, with trepidation to hide the volume I was reading. A knock, and the door was opened ere I could reply. Arnetage entered, as I half expected, yet most feared, thinking it impossible. He sat himself heavily down, and I observed that his face was stern and rigid, the noble features having an exaggerated appearance, as if carved in marble; he was worn to a shadow and looked shockingly ill. His first word—"Margaret?"

"She is well," said I, with such nervous eagerness that I seemed to make of the words but one syllable. I had with unconsciousness, and by some instinct, spoken as if he had not read, and I had not written, the letters of her illness and death. The next moment I recollected them, and this added excessive confusion to my manner. He looked at me as if I were very far off, his brow deepened in sternness, and he broke a long silence in a deep measured tone:—

"I half guess how it is; so will ask no more now, but tell you at once why you see me, and why you see me thus. My last letter told you that I was about to sail for Italy. Since then, if you have written, I have received no letters, and no wonder, for I never reached the destination I pointed out to you. To Italy I went, but it seems that I carried with me the seeds of the plague from the Greek islands; and instead of proceeding inland at once, I was forced to wait for some weeks ill of a terrible fever. I found myself dreadfully weakened when the fever left me; and the physicians said that the most speedy way to recover a degree of strength would be to remain quiet by the seaside. So in a small and most glossy vale, on the Adriatic coast, I took a cottage wherein to live in quiet. I must be particular in describing this place. It had one chief room, which I converted into a bedroom, with two windows, almost opposite each other, and opening east and west, as the cottage itself fronted seaward and shoreward. In this room weakness compelled me to lie during a great part of the day, gazing sadly and impotently from these two windows. From the west window I could behold one of the most beautiful of Italian landscapes—a long level tract rising inland, cornfield and pasture and vineyard, islanded by huge rocks and dark-stemmed, dark-tufted trees, rising slowly beyond and beyond one another until they ceased in scarcely seen mountains. Before this window and close at hand were two large twin beech trees, whose shadows at sunset and moonset fell forwards across my room and across my bed. From the east window I could see the clear Adriatic rising and sinking in its tides without a ripple: yet this sea too, could look wan and ghostly beneath the moon.

"Here then I remained until I had mustered strength to walk along the beach, upon the sand beneath the high pile of rounded stones stretching far away leagues long, curving with the curved shore, which even this calm sea had been heaping up during the ages of its being. I had also penetrated inland for some distance among the vines and olives, and might have prolonged my stay until recovered health made me really fit for departure, but it was not to be so.

"One evening I had been watching with pleasure the long strokes of the sunset upon the rows of vines that ran down towards the shore, how the light caught the heads of the branches and flung them in shadow upon one another, and how the strong shore-grass danced and glanced almost like steel for brightness. These and other things now forgotten had I been watching, and thought sweetly the while of Margaret, of you, and of home. It was an evening of unusual peace and blessedness, and I thought of it again when I went to bed, and again was happy.

"But that night I dreamt that the moon was rising over the waters in great lustre, so that the whole sea was living, and defined with rolling golden light, all except one tract far, far to the east, behind the moon, where there seemed to be a residue of mist and infinite space. Out of this there emerged, suddenly, and with great swiftness, coming towards me,—I was standing on the shore, above that ridge of smooth round boulders, a large dark object, which I could not at first make out. It neared and neared, however, with inconceivable rapidity, until I was able to discover what it was. It was a large two-masted vessel, but with only the stumps of its masts remaining, and without a scrap of canvass, or rigging, or gear of any sort to be seen about it. Without any visible propulsion it was moving straight and swift for the shore just where I stood. Close above it, and exactly accompanying it, flew a black cloud, sending forth rain in long undiminishing streams, until the deck-planking was soaked, and torrents were pouring from the ports. The sky above was cloudless and serene. Upon the deck of this strange ship appeared two figures—a man at the helm deeply muffled, and in the bows a lady kneeling, whose features I somehow could not discern, although her face was uncovered, and her hair thrown back lank and dripping. I made out, however, that she wore an aspect of deadly pallor, and I remember that I thought she was sea-sick. All this I had time to make out; for, though the whole thing came on without abating an instant of its fearful speed, yet there was an enormous interval of time between my first recognizing what it was and its approaching very nearly. But suddenly it seemed only a few yards distant, steadily holding on its course. I shouted to the helmsman to beware, but my voice only muttered in my own ears. I saw the water between it and the shore slightly agitated; the next moment the huge black bows had lifted against the ridge of boulders, and were grinding and groaning upon it. I rushed down to aid the lady; but at my first step she vanished flutteringly towards the sea, like the spray of a fountain caught and drifted by the wind. The steersman lingered a little, standing on one leg; then, with contortions altogether unusual, he jerked himself over the side of the vessel. I awoke struggling to scale the ship, which yielded to my weight.

"I awoke startled, and saw the moon sinking, and the two beech trees, with the moon behind them, tossing and nodding towards me with huge plumes, and many a ghastly chasm among their leaves, through which lolled long inane faces, open-mouthed, mocking me. Then I saw that the fantastic shadow dance of their leaves was flickering on the floor, and up to my bed. And it came upon me that she whom I had seen was, could be, no other than Margaret, and that I had indeed seen a vision, a portent summoning me away. The impression remained strong in the morning, though I had slept again; and I did not try to reason it away, but set forth straightway homewards, obeying destiny; and am here, expecting anything, fully able to bear anything, should it be that Margaret is dead."

Thus a dream had power to work upon the habitually, though calmly, enthusiastic temperament of my friend.

"My brother, my brother," I cried, as Arnetage paused, "it is so: let it be for both of us."

He took the announcement calmly, as if he had been long nerved to it, and patiently inquired into the circumstances of her illness and death. We sat very late that night, and next morning he was to go on to our native town. And that night, partly to divert his sorrow, partly to relieve myself of an intolerable burden, I told him the story of my own love for Margaret, concealing nothing. I knew that it was selfish to obtrude my own miseries upon him then; but he was so calm, so majestic in his self-control, and the weight hung so heavy upon me that I could not refrain; and I was afterwards glad that I obeyed the impulse. He wept at my tale,—he who had shed no tear for himself; and I felt, as I concluded, that the old hysterical agony had ceased within me, never to revive, and that I could henceforth hold converse with the memory of Margaret in unsullied and abiding love. We ascertained that the day and hour of the vision corresponded closely with the time of Margaret's decease.

Arnetage went into the world, sternly and uncompromisingly fulfilling every duty. We were inseparable; we often talked unreservedly of Margaret, and imperceptibly my soul grew more and more attuned to his heroic pitch. But ever he grew paler and thinner; and one word of solemn prophecy was ever on his unmoved lips. "He who hath seen a spirit, a spirit shall soon become." True, for within the year he was lying by the side of Margaret.

I am now alone upon earth—alone in the midst of men, alone in converse with those two blessed ones, whom I see in heaven; but whether my time here be long or short, matters nothing.